D1505526

MYSTERY OF THE FLYING EXPRESS

A sleek new hydrofoil is scheduled to start ferrying passengers between Bayport and Cape Cutlass. But business enemies of the hydrofoil owner have stirred up a hornets' nest of violent opposition among small boat owners. Fearing sabotage, he begs Frank and Joe Hardy to guard the *Flying Express* on her maiden trip.

Startling developments plunge the teen-age detectives into a dangerous chase by sea, air, and land in pursuit of a gang of hardened criminals who operate by the signs of the Zodiac. The Hardys' close pal Chet Morton tries to help them by using his newly acquired knowledge of astrology.

Tension mounts when the *Flying Express* vanishes— and so does Sam Radley, Mr. Hardy's skilled operative. Has Radley been kidnapped? Is he a prisoner aboard the stolen hydrofoil? Peril stalks Frank and Joe's every move as they hunt down the terrifying gangleader Zodiac Zig and his vicious henchmen.

The hydrofoil plowed into the boat amidships!

Hardy Boys Mystery Stories

MYSTERY OF THE FLYING EXPRESS

BY

FRANKLIN W. DIXON

NEW YORK
GROSSET & DUNLAP
A NATIONAL GENERAL COMPANY
Publishers

CONTENTS

MYSTERY OF THE FLYING EXPRESS

CHAPTER I

Stargazer

LOUD explosions, like a fusillade of gunfire, echoed through the quiet streets of Bayport. An old jalopy careened around the corner. The driver, plump and freckle-faced, pulled up before the home of Fenton Hardy, private detective.

Frank Hardy, eighteen years old, and his brother Joe, a year younger, guessed who was coming before they spotted their visitor.

"Chet Morton, for sure," said blond-haired Joe, looking out a window. "And is he excited!"

Chet waved and beckoned. "Hey, fellows! Big doings at the waterfront! Let's go!" he called out as the Hardy boys bounded down the front steps.

"What is it all about?" asked dark-haired Frank.

"Hop in and I'll explain on the way."

The three crowded into the front seat. Chet started the car, which lurched away from the

1

curb, jouncing its passengers as it picked up speed and headed for Bayport Harbor.

Joe braced himself with a hand against the dashboard. "Okay, we're on our way. You'd better clue us in before this ancient heap decides to pause for a rest!"

Chet chuckled. "Sir, you are referring to the vehicle I love, but I'll overlook the remark in view of the circumstances! Seriously, though, there's real trouble down there. Something to do with the big hydrofoil."

Joe looked surprised. "The *Flying Express?* I thought she was all set for her maiden spin the day after tomorrow."

Chet shifted gears as he turned onto Bayport's main street. "Right. She's scheduled to begin her new commuter service to Providence. Wish I had a ticket, but they're all sold out."

Providence was a port at the tip of Cape Cutlass, seventy miles south of Bayport. The three youths often spun down there and back aboard the Hardys' motorboat, the *Sleuth.*

"What's wrong with the *Flying Express?"* Frank wanted to know. "Mechanical failure?"

"Not the way I understand it," Chet replied. "Something to do with public relations. Seems that quite a few people would like to foil the hydrofoil!"

"Ow!" Joe said. "Pretty corny pun."

Chet stopped at a red light near Condor's Photo Store. "Hey, Frank, let's pick up the passport pictures while we're here," Joe suggested.

"Good idea. Chet, pull over for a minute, will you?"

Fenton Hardy and his operative Sam Radley had had their photos taken to renew their passports, which were always kept up to date. Chet parked in front of the shop and the Hardys hastened inside. Frank took Sam's pictures, while Joe pocketed his father's. They paid the photographer and soon were off again for the waterfront.

As they approached the dock where the *Flying Express* was berthed they could hear the tumult of the crowd gathered there. Small boat owners milled around, shouting and gesturing at the shiny white fiberglass vessel riding low in the water. Chet parked the car nearby and they all got out.

The ship's sleek hull had enclosed cabins forward and aft, and a rakish pilot's bridge. The windshields of the wheelhouse looked out over a metal deck. This forward deck obviously was not for passengers. The rear deck was slightly lower and guarded by white pipe railing.

"Quite a boat," Frank said admiringly.

"She's a hundred feet long and has accommodations for sixty passengers," Chet explained, "with a top speed of seventy miles an hour."

"I wonder what they have against a beauty like that," Joe said, pointing toward a picket line carrying placards. In bold lettering one sign read:

STOP THE FLYING EXPRESS
MAKE BARMET BAY SAFE

"Beats me," Frank replied. "I can't see that she'll get in anybody's way as long as she slows down when she enters the harbor. Barmet Bay's big enough for everybody."

Chet had been inspecting the rest of the crowd. "Those kids near the slip are painting signs. I think I'll mosey over for a closer look at their artistic productions— Hey, what's this?"

One of the sign painters suddenly pushed a placard into his hand. Frank and Joe received the same treatment from a couple of paint-smeared teen-agers. Before they realized it, the Hardys and Chet were holding slogans of protest against the hydrofoil.

"Say, we have nothing to do with you guys!" Chet shouted angrily.

"Watch it!" Joe warned. "Here comes a TV news truck! Let's get out of here!"

Hurriedly the boys threw down the placards. But it was too late! The truck had swept past, its lens pointing directly at them!

"Holy catfish! They got us!" Joe groaned.

Some of the pickets were yelling for a raid on the *Flying Express*. "Scuttle the hydrofoil!" one of them shouted. The rest took up the chant: "Scuttle the hydrofoil! Scuttle the hydrofoil!"

They were about to go into action when a police car rolled into the middle of the mob. Bayport's chief of police got out and surveyed the disorder.

"We've got a complaint about this dock being blocked illegally," Chief Collig boomed through a bullhorn. "I want some explanations. Let's start with you two fellows— Well, if it isn't Frank and Joe Hardy! How did you get involved?"

Chief Collig knew the Hardy boys well because they frequently helped their father with his detective cases. Their ability as amateur sleuths was known to practically everyone in Bayport, and they cooperated with the police whenever they could.

While Frank spoke to the chief, Chet slipped away to a group of sign painters, and began working with a brush and a piece of cardboard.

"Some pal, leaving us to face the music," Joe thought.

"We're not in this fracas, Chief!" Frank said. "We're the most innocent bystanders you ever saw."

A middle-aged woman rushed forward brandishing a finger at the Hardys. "Innocent my foot. I saw them! They were right in the middle of it."

Chet, carrying a sign behind his back, edged his way into the group around Frank and Joe.

The woman was running out of breath. She finished by pointing to a placard on the ground, and declared triumphantly, "There, that's one of the signs they were carrying! Look for yourself."

"I'll get it," Chet said quickly. Stooping, he deftly switched placards and straightened up with the one he had been carrying. He pushed it into Frank's hand, and raised the boy's elbow so that everybody could read the words he had painted:

FRANK HARDY FOR MAYOR

A roar of laughter came from the crowd. Even Chief Collig showed the trace of a smile.

Frank glanced at the sign and winked at Chet.

By now the ugly mood of the protestors was evaporating. They began to drift away from the dock. Seeing that everything was under control, Chief Collig drove back to headquarters.

Frank, Joe, and Chet returned to the Hardy home. They were met at the door by the boys' Aunt Gertrude, Fenton Hardy's sister, who had come to live with the family some time ago. She was tall, angular, and had a no-nonsense look behind her spectacles. Although Aunt Gertrude scolded the boys for taking what she considered too many risks, she held her nephews in deepest affection.

"I hear there has been trouble at the waterfront," she said sternly. "No doubt you were there!"

A roar of laughter came from the crowd

"Of course we were, Aunty." Joe grinned. "But we spent most of our time with Chief Collig—on the right side of the law!"

Chet rolled his eyes at Aunt Gertrude. "How's the food situation today? You wouldn't happen to have any of my favorite pies in the house, would you?"

"Maybe I would, Chet. Come on into the kitchen!"

While she put big slices of rhubarb-and-strawberry pie on three plates, Frank took milk from the refrigerator. Then the trio carried their refreshments into the living room.

"You know," Chet remarked between mouthfuls, "I still don't know how a hydrofoil works."

"At slow speeds, it floats on the surface like a boat," Frank explained. "When the pilot revs up the motor, the hull rises clear of the water and skims along like a low flying aircraft. Neat invention, made by Enrico Forlanini in 1906."

"You mean it actually takes off?" Chet asked.

"No. It never loses contact with the water because it stands on struts attached to submerged foils. They are shaped like wings to give a balancing effect."

"I think I get it."

"You see, Chet," Frank continued, "as speed increases, the water flowing over the rounded top of the foils travels faster than the water underneath. That causes less pressure above, and gives the hull the lift to get clear of the surface. Same principle as a plane in the air."

Chet downed his last piece of pie. "What about propulsion?"

Joe took up the explanation. "The U. S. Navy has done a great deal of experimenting, using everything from gasoline to jet engines. The *Flying Express* happens to be diesel-powered. The motor turns the screw propellers at the stern. A hydrofoil provides a fast, smooth ride, and it doesn't create much of a wake."

"Exactly," Frank pointed out. "So why should the small boat owners object to a hydrofoil on Barmet Bay? It's not going to swamp them. Accidents will happen, but you can say that of anything that sails. Today's protest was mystifying, to say the least."

Joe sighed. "You said it. Anyhow, it's too bad we won't be aboard on her first trip. We had planned to take Callie and Iola, but went for tickets too late."

Callie Shaw was Frank's favorite date, and Joe enjoyed being with Chet's sister Iola.

Chet put his glass down with a clank. "Jumping Gemini! I could have told you to save your time and energy. You and Callie are both Aries. Your horoscopes indicate that bad news is all you can expect right now since you were born under the sign of the Ram!"

Frank and Joe exchanged knowing smiles. Chet

was always involved in some new hobby. Just now it was astrology—casting horoscopes to discover the influence that the stars and planets are supposed to have upon a person's life.

"So you're reading Joe's fate in the stars?" Frank joshed.

"Don't laugh." Chet spoke with an owlish air of solemnity. "You're Scorpio. The sign of the Scorpion. The planets aren't in the right conjunction for you this month either!"

"Do you really believe all that?"

"Sure I do. What was good enough for the ancient Egyptians is good enough for me."

Chet adopted the tone of a professor lecturing to rather dimwitted students. It was a pose he enjoyed. "Listen carefully. A Scorpion likes to think things out, taking into account all the factors of a problem. He's good at analyzing clues and motives. He's a born leader. That's you, Frank."

Chet cleared his throat and went on, "An Arian is more of an activist. He dashes into all kinds of situations without worrying too much about consequences. He's full of enthusiasm and good humor. That's you, Joe. Makes sense, doesn't it?"

The Hardys agreed that it did. On many of their cases, Frank tended to be the leader because he could figure out the logical steps to take. Joe, on the other hand, was impetuous and refused to admit anything was impossible.

"Still," Frank mused, "there are times when I'm more impulsive and—"

"Hey. Looks as if we're getting company," Joe interrupted his brother.

The other two boys joined Joe at the window. A man stopped and looked at the Hardy house. He strode past, turned around, paused, and squinted at the number again. Then he approached the front door.

"Here comes more bad news!" Chet quavered.

CHAPTER II

First Warning

THE bell rang. Joe headed for the door and admitted the stranger.

"I'm looking for Frank and Joe Hardy," the man said.

"I'm Joe. Come on inside."

Joe escorted the visitor into the living room and introduced Frank and Chet. The man seemed a bit jumpy, as if his nerves were on edge. He shifted his weight from one foot to the other, and twisted the brim of his felt hat between his fingers.

"My name is Spencer Given," he began. "I'm here because I want you boys to ride on the *Flying Express* for a few runs, starting the day after tomorrow!"

Frank and Joe stared at each other in surprise. "Are you kidding?" Frank said. "We tried to get tickets days ago. They're all sold out!"

12

"Don't joke," Given replied. "I happen to own the hydrofoil. And I'd like to hire you as detectives!"

Frank raised his eyebrows. "You expect trouble?"

"Well, the small boat owners of Bayport, the railroad, and the bus companies all resent the competition. That's why they spread the rumor that the *Flying Express* wasn't safe and that was the reason for the demonstration down at the dock today."

Frank nodded. "We know."

"Completely unfair!" Given exploded wrathfully. "Boats on Barmet Bay won't be in any danger from my craft. And I won't be taking any substantial number of patrons away from the trains and buses. Yet they won't listen. They're determined to drive me off the run to Cape Cutlass."

The boys listened with growing interest.

"I don't believe they'd stop at anything," Given continued. "What's got me worried is the possibility of sabotage—those foils and propellers are vulnerable.

"That's why I want you on board. You could circulate among the passengers and keep your eyes open. If you spotted anyone up to mischief, you could blow the whistle on him."

Frank pinched his lower lip. "I don't know," he said doubtfully. "Since you're looking for a detective, why didn't you contact my father? Dad's an old master at sabotage cases."

"Fenton Hardy would be ideal," Given admitted, "but he's too high-priced for this assignment. Amateurs should be able to handle it. I want you two fellows because I've checked your records. You're pretty good detectives who've cracked quite a few cases."

The boys' accomplishments in crime detection were almost as well known as those of their famous father. Their first success was solving the mystery of *The Tower Treasure,* and their recent adventure was known as *The Disappearing Floor.*

Frank turned to his brother. "What do you think, Joe?"

"I'm all for it," Joe declared enthusiastically. He turned to Chet. "Want to give us a hand?"

Chet looked doubtful. "This—er—saboteur won't be able to blow up the boat or something drastic like that, will he?"

Frank chuckled. "That's what we're hired for. To prevent any funny business he might have in mind. Well, Chet, you want to come or not?"

"Sure, sure. Somebody's got to look after you!"

"Another point," Joe put in. "Our girl friends would never forgive us if we traveled to Cape Cutlass without them. Do you think you could get us a couple of extra tickets, Mr. Given?"

Given wagged his head approvingly. "That's not a bad idea! With your girls along no one will suspect that you're there for any other purpose than the joy-ride. But I don't want you to pay all your attention to the girls, now. Remember, you've got a job to do!"

"Don't worry," Frank said. "We'll be on the ball."

Given sighed in relief and extended a hand. "It's a deal."

Just then footsteps were heard on the stairs and Aunt Gertrude bustled into the living room. When she saw Given, she stopped short.

Frank introduced their visitor. "Aunt Gertrude, this is Mr. Given. He owns the hydrofoil."

"Oh," Aunt Gertrude said. "How do you do? I was just about to tune in the five-o'clock news. There might be something on the waterfront trouble. You don't mind, do you?"

"No, of course not," Given said as she snapped on the television set.

Frank and Joe exchanged appalled glances, remembering how the TV camera had isolated them in the midst of the anti-hydrofoil picketers. What would Given think of that? Better ease him out of the house pronto!

"No need for us to hold you any longer, Mr. Given," Frank hinted broadly.

"Here's your hat, Mr. Given," Chet said quickly.

"Let me show you to the door, Mr. Given," Joe offered as calmly as he could.

Their visitor started to leave but turned back to the living room. "Come to think of it, I'd better hear the news too. The trouble your aunt mentioned is of great concern to me. Let's see if they show the *Flying Express* on the screen."

"Good night, we're sunk!" Joe whispered to Frank.

Too late to do anything about it now! The camera swept across the milling crowd on the dock, then focused on a group of three—Frank, Joe, and Chet! Each was holding an anti-hydrofoil placard!

Spencer Given turned purple with rage. "You were with the pickets trying to run me out of business!" he shouted. "And to think I offered you a job! Well, you fooled me once, but never again! The deal's off!"

"Mr. Given," Frank pleaded, "this wasn't our fault. Somebody pushed those signs—"

The TV picture changed to Chet doing his sleight-of-hand with the placards. In a moment he was holding up Frank's arm. The lettering on the placard could be seen clearly:

FRANK HARDY FOR MAYOR

Aunt Gertrude chuckled at the antics of her nephews and their friend. "I think you owe the boys an apology, Mr. Given," she said.

"Well, perhaps I do," Given said sheepishly. "For a moment I thought somebody was stabbing me in the back. Anyway, the deal's on as far as I'm concerned."

The boys nodded their agreement.

All the while Chet had been sizing up the caller. Suddenly he blurted, "Mr. Given, when's your birthday?"

The question took the boat owner by surprise. "What's that got to do with my hydrofoil?"

"It might have a lot to—" Chet began, but Given was impatient.

"Cut the comedy," he said and turned away.

Aunt Gertrude chuckled and said, "Now I'm curious, Chester," she said. "Mr. Given, please give the boy your birth date!"

"March first," Given grumbled.

Chet clucked sympathetically. "Too bad! You're a Pisces, governed by the sign of the Fishes. That bodes ill at this phase of the moon!"

"Bah, what nonsense!" Given shook his head in disgust, said good-by to Aunt Gertrude, pulled on his hat, and left.

"I don't think he takes your astrology very seriously, Chet," Joe remarked with a laugh.

"Not as seriously as he takes his hydrofoil. That's for sure," Frank observed.

"But they go together!" Chet protested. "The unfavorable conjunction of the heavenly bodies relates to everything he does—and that includes his commuter service to Cape Cutlass. There's a lot of trouble ahead for Given."

Gertrude Hardy had been listening with mounting interest. "Chet Morton, what's all this about you taking up astrology? Can you really cast horoscopes? How about mine?"

"Sure, Aunt Gertrude. But it takes time to read the stars. I can tell you a few things right off the bat, though. Day and month of birth, please."

"Well, since you're not asking for the year, I don't mind telling you that I was born on August twenty-fifth. Which sign is that?"

Chet gulped, blushed, and evaded the gaze of his questioner.

"You— You're a—a beautiful young goddess!" he stammered.

Aunt Gertrude blushed. "Chet Morton, you're impossible!"

"Well, it's Virgo, the sign of the Virgin," Chet said lamely.

Aunt Gertrude smoothed her hair with one hand. "Go on!"

Chet continued the analysis. "Virgos have great analytical ability. They know how to get to the heart of important matters without wasting time on inconsequential details. They're also sensitive persons who enjoy dealing with other people, and they prefer the simple life. They talk a lot, which is all right because they often have something to say that's really worthwhile."

Miss Hardy looked pleased.

"The stars insist you'd make a good critic or perhaps a repairman!" Chet went on.

Miss Hardy looked at him through her steel-rimmed spectacles and giggled. "Thank you, Chet. I can't say that I'm charmed by that repairman bit! The rest, however, is quite satisfactory. If every horoscope you draw up is as complimentary as mine, you'll have more friends than you need."

Chet grinned.

"I'll see that you get a big slice of my angel food cake as a reward," Aunt Gertrude concluded as she pushed through the swinging door to the kitchen.

"How about your own horoscope, Chet?" Joe inquired teasingly.

"I'm Cancer. The sign of the Crab. You fellows can probably guess that I'm fated to be a good cook! The signs haven't been on my side recently, but I'm happy to report that a change is coming. The moon and the Crab . . ."

The ringing of the phone interrupted Chet. Joe picked it up. An unfamiliar voice came through.

"Hardy?"

"Joe Hardy speaking."

"I have a message for you and your brother."

"Go ahead." Joe motioned Frank and Chet to put their ears close to the receiver.

"We've heard about you gadflies. Take a friendly word of advice. If you're smart, you'll have nothing more to do with Spencer Given. Turn down whatever deal he offered you and get out while you're still in one piece."

"Who are you?" Joe demanded.

"Never mind. And by the way, don't ride on the *Flying Express*. It's dangerous!"

The man hung up.

CHAPTER III

Hot Merchandise

"Leaping Libras!" Chet blurted out. "Who was that?"

Joe replaced the instrument. "No way of telling." He frowned. "But he doesn't like Hardy and Company."

"Still he wasn't really interested in us," Frank said. "His purpose was to give a warning about the *Flying Express*. I've a hunch he's one of Spencer Given's enemies."

"Could be," Joe said. "Probably tailed Given to our house, figured out a deal was in the offing, and made his move to scare us off before we got near the hydrofoil. He must have phoned from somewhere near the house after he saw Given leave."

"The corner phone booth two blocks away!" Frank exclaimed. "He may still be there!"

The three raced out of the house and down the

street. They were a block away from the phone booth when the doors folded inward. They saw a flash of blond hair and a maroon dress on the figure that emerged, slipped hurriedly into a foreign sports car, and sped off.

"Well, I'll be a monkey's uncle! It's a woman!" Joe gasped. "But the caller sounded like a man!"

"Maybe she has a deep voice," Frank said. "Let's see if she left any clues to her identity."

The Hardys gave the booth a rapid once-over without finding anything. Then Chet went in, flipped open the coin return slot, and extracted a dime.

"Jupiter is fully aligned with Uranus!" He chuckled. "No wonder my luck has changed! If it holds up from here on out, I'll only need a one-way ticket to Cape Cutlass!"

"Now what does that mean?" Frank inquired.

"Can't tell you yet," Chet replied mysteriously. "My horoscope says I'd better stay mum for the time being. I'll let you in on it when the signs are more favorable."

Joe, who had been scrutinizing the area, bent over and plucked something from the gutter. He held the object up with a significant wink. It was a thick cigar butt, still burning. The other end was smudged with lipstick.

"That was no lady," he quipped. "It was a man with a taste for smelly black stogies."

Frank nodded. "Pretty clever way to trail friend

Given. He's in a tizzy about boatmen and trainmen and bus drivers. But he wouldn't suspect a blonde in a sports car."

Chet looked worried. He realized that the threat was not an idle one. And Chet had an aversion to danger, even though the Hardys could always count on him when help was needed.

"Maybe he or she or whatever it was will blow up the *Flying Express* after all," he said. "Do you suppose we should get the police in on it?"

"No. Given certainly doesn't want that. It would be bad publicity for his boat. Also, there's nothing definite to base a complaint on," Frank decided.

"You're not getting cold feet, are you, Chet?" Joe teased.

"Who, me? Of course not."

"All right, then let's go on with the game."

That evening Fenton Hardy returned home. He was surprised to learn that his sons had made a deal with Spencer Given to guard the *Flying Express.*

"I've heard about the man," Mr. Hardy said. "He's a shrewd operator. Speculates in real estate and hopes he can trigger a land boom on Cape Cutlass by means of his hydrofoil. You can see why he's concerned. He's staking a fortune on the success of the *Flying Express.*"

"He must have quite a bit of money," Frank put in.

"He does. But he's known to be rather stingy."

Frank and Joe laughed. "We noticed that. He told us that he couldn't afford to hire *you*. That's why we got the job."

Mr. Hardy grinned. "Well, you know what you're doing. No doubt you'll have an exciting ride to Providence. Just keep an eye open for that wolf in disguise you mentioned, or it might be too exciting for comfort."

"We will," Joe promised.

"Meanwhile, I'm leaving for Shark Island. The State Police have asked me to track down a gang who specialize in stripping small craft. They're clever pros with a profitable gimmick."

"What is it?" Joe asked eagerly.

"It seems that first they go around taking orders for engines, props, radios, anything needed to keep a boat operating in the water," Mr. Hardy said. "Then they case the shoreline for unprotected boats."

"What a racket!" Frank reflected. "Satisfaction guaranteed! Orders filled right on time with hot merchandise!"

"That's about the size of it," Mr. Hardy concurred. "They haven't gotten this far north yet, so I'm going down to Shark Island to do some undercover work."

"That's about fifty miles below Cape Cutlass, isn't it?" Joe asked.

"Right. It seems like a logical lair for the gang, especially since most of the activity is going on around there."

"Dad, maybe we can help you," Frank suggested. "We'll only be tied up with Given for a few runs!"

"There's not much you boys can do for me at this point in the case. I won't have a clear picture until I've snooped around Shark Island. However, it would be a good idea for you to keep in touch. Here's my phone number." Mr. Hardy handed Frank a slip of paper.

"Also," he went on, "you'd better activate the electronic beeper on the *Sleuth*. Even though there haven't been any thefts up here yet, the gang might expand at any time."

Frank nodded. "And we certainly don't want to lose our boat!"

Mrs. Hardy packed her husband's bag. She was a slender, pretty woman who had long since learned what a detective needed in the field. Disguises, bugging devices, emergency rations—all went into the suitcase before she snapped it shut.

Shortly afterward Fenton Hardy was on his way to Shark Island.

At breakfast the next morning the phone rang. Joe reached for the instrument with suppressed excitement. "If it's Dad, perhaps he's got an assignment for us already!"

The voice of Chet Morton bubbled through the receiver. "Guess what? Lady Luck is really smiling today. I've got a job!"

"No kidding? As an astrologer?" Joe asked.

"Of course not. I wanted to work for the summer, so I had applied at the Starfish Marina in Cape Cutlass a while ago. Naturally I didn't expect any answer while the Cancerian conjunctions weren't right."

Joe whistled. "I see. But now they are?"

"Yes sir. The moon is marching on through the Zodiac. The owner phoned and told me to report immediately. That's what I meant yesterday when I said I might only need a one-way ticket."

"Well, that's great, Chet. But what about our sleuthing on the hydrofoil? If you're leaving right away—"

"Who said I won't wait till tomorrow?" Chet pretended to be hurt. "I promised you I'd come along. I'm a man of my word!"

"Okay. We'll see you in the morning, then."

Frank and Joe started out early the next day to pick up their friends. Callie and Iola were waiting in front of the Morton farm.

"Chet left already," Iola called out. "He said he had some sleuthing work to do—on his own!"

The two girls were attractive in different ways. Iola Morton, a brunette, had mobile features, sparkling eyes, and a lot of vitality. She was wearing a pink suit. Callie Shaw was blond, tall, and slender. She wore a yellow skirt and striped jacket.

As they were driving toward the dock, Iola remarked, "I think it was just swell of you boys to invite us along on the *Flying Express*."

"I think so, too," Callie declared. "How did you ever manage to get the tickets?"

Joe did the explaining while Frank drove. Callie sat up straight, her hands in her lap, and stated primly, "Well, we might have known! Whenever Frank and Joe take us out, we're bound to end up in the middle of a mystery!"

"I'm not complaining." Iola laughed. "A ride on the *Flying Express* is worth a mystery!"

Frank parked the car and the four got into the line of passengers boarding the hydrofoil. Joe presented the tickets that Spencer Given had provided, and they stepped onto the deck.

Everything was new and shiny, an attractive combination of fiberglass, chromium, and highly polished wood. The pilot, a salty man about thirty, sat behind the wheel. Given stood beside him, beaming with satisfaction.

"I hope Chet gets here on time," Joe remarked. "Didn't he tell you anything about where he was going?"

Iola shook her head. "No. He said he'd meet us on the *Flying Express*. He was sure he wouldn't have any trouble getting aboard, since Given invited him."

Frank and Joe walked around the narrow rear deck while Callie and Iola stepped down into the long cabin, where comfortable seats were arranged in rows on either side of a center aisle. The passengers were chatting gaily, but Chet was not among them.

Finally the Hardys came inside. "Chet didn't make the scene," Frank reported.

As he spoke, the engine started with a muffled roar and the *Flying Express* began to move. Slowly it churned away from the pier and out into Barmet Bay.

"Chet's got me worried," Joe said anxiously as the waves flashed by more quickly.

The hull rose above the surface of the water and the foils beneath came into view. Soon the *Flying Express* was skimming at top speed out across the bay on its way to Providence.

"Certainly no sabotage on that take-off," Iola commented with a thrill in her voice.

"So far so good," Joe agreed. "If the rest of the trip is like this, Mr. Given should be a happy man by the time we get to Cape Cutlass."

Frank rubbed his cheek. "That's where we come in. It's our business to see that the *Flying Express* does have a smooth trip. The take-off is only the beginning. There'll be many more chances for sabotage farther down the bay."

He turned to the girls. "You two can enjoy yourselves while we have a look-see. Joe, suppose you take the bow and find out if anything's stirring. I'll take the stern. We can compare notes afterward."

Iola and Callie settled into comfortable lounge seats. Joe went forward. Everything seemed peaceful throughout the vessel.

Frank stepped onto a catwalk at the stern. The wind buffeted him and he had to hang onto the railing. Below him a foil hissed along the surface and the propellers kicked up white foam. Fascinated by the hydrofoil's principle of physics, he leaned over for a better look.

Suddenly Frank sensed someone creeping up behind him. He tried to dodge. Too late! A pair of hands struck him heavily between the shoulders, flipping him over the side!

Down he plunged toward the protruding foil —and toward the churning propeller beneath it!

CHAPTER IV

A Near Miss

WILDLY Frank threw his arms out. His hands clutched the upper end of the foil and braked his descent.

For a moment he teetered there, straining every muscle to save himself from falling onto the deadly propeller, whirling like a buzz saw only a few feet below. His grip held! Frank pulled himself against the foil. He wrapped his arms tightly around it, lifting his feet clear of the foaming water which tore at his body. His shouts for help were soundless in the din.

How long could his strength endure? The foil was slippery under his fingers because of the spray washing over it. Desperately Frank tried to hold on. But his grip was beginning to weaken! He started to slide down the foil toward the water! In a moment he would be caught in the propeller!

Frantically he glanced up, and with hazy vision

was amazed to see a girl looking down. Spotting Frank half in the water, she froze momentarily, then shouted for help.

"Man overboard! Man overboard!"

Joe had gone to the stern to join Frank. He had just climbed to the rear deck when he heard the warning cry. Instinctively he knew that Frank was in trouble and rushed to alert the pilot, who cut the power.

The propellers stopped whirling and the *Flying Express* settled slowly to a stop in the middle of the bay. Joe and the pilot lowered a line and Frank was pulled onto the deck.

"Just in time," Frank gasped as he sat down, exhausted.

Spencer Given pushed through the knot of gawking passengers. His face showed the familiar tinge of purple that the boys had noticed the day he had come to the Hardys' house.

"What's the meaning of this?" he fumed. "You might have damaged my boat!"

"Mr. Given," Frank protested, "your boat might have damaged me! It was touch-and-go down there!"

"Is this any time for joking? How's the foil and the propeller?" Given asked. Told that they were in good working condition, he stalked back to the bridge.

"Real huff he's in," Joe remarked.

"I guess he has a right to be," Frank said in a

low voice. "A detective should know better than to go up on a catwalk alone when he suspects there's a saboteur on the prowl. We're here to prevent trouble not to invite it."

He stood up shakily as the engine sent vibrations along the metal deck. "By the way, where's the girl who gave the alarm? I'd like to tell her how grateful I am."

They inquired among the passengers, but no one had noticed the girl.

"Was she pretty?" Callie asked, sounding a trifle jealous.

"I didn't have time to notice," Frank replied.

The crowd dispersed slowly and the young detectives stepped down into the rear cabin.

By now the *Flying Express* had picked up speed again. The passengers were relieved that the man overboard had been rescued so quickly.

But they were greatly disturbed by the incident. Complaints and criticism flew back and forth. Would they get to Cape Cutlass on time? No one knew. Would they get there at all?

The hydrofoil passed dozens of small craft sailing the bay or riding at anchor. The appearance of the big boat caused a sensation. Boys and girls cheered. Women waved gaily colored handkerchiefs. But quite a few skippers shook their fists and glared as the *Flying Express* flashed by.

Spencer Given came up behind the Hardys while they were viewing the spectacle. "There!"

he erupted violently. "See those fellows on that launch shaking their fists at us? That's the kind of thing I have to expect. Stay on guard! This trip's not over by a long shot! We can't trust anybody who navigates anything on Barmet Bay!"

"What about anybody who flies over Barmet Bay?" Joe pointed at a plane overhead. "That guy in the sky is definitely playing tag. He's been following us right down the bay, sticking to us like a guided missile homing in on target."

"Wonder what's he up to?" Frank asked.

The pilot provided the answer. Lining his plane up, with the hydrofoil about a mile astern, he gave it the gun, and swooped down.

"That plane's going to crash into us!" someone shouted in terror. Panic broke out. There was a headlong dash for the exit.

With jaws clenched Frank and Joe waited for the impact, holding on firmly to Callie and Iola.

"Oh, Joe, I'm so scared!" Iola shuddered.

At the last possible moment the pilot leveled out. The plane roared over the hydrofoil from stern to bow, coming so close that the sounds of its engines were deafening.

"No markings!" Joe registered the fact instantaneously. "They must be covered with tape, otherwise they'd be clearly visible at the altitude that fellow flies!"

Frank nudged him and pointed to the bottom of the fuselage where a heavy wooden log was fastened with clamps just behind the wheels. The next second the clamps opened and the log plummeted into the sea directly in front of the speeding hydrofoil!

The skipper of the *Flying Express* twisted the wheel and swung his craft sharply to one side. Some passengers were knocked down; others slid off the seats.

The big boat shuddered as it turned, but the pilot pulled her bow away from the log. It grazed and bumped the foils on one side, then disappeared astern.

"Quick thinking by the fellow in the wheelhouse!" Frank exclaimed. "If we'd hit that log, the hull might have been staved!"

"There goes the plane! No hope of identifying him now!" Joe said. "Well, I'd better let Dad know about this incident. I can contact him on Shark Island through the ship's radiotelephone."

Mr. Hardy answered the call. Joe related Frank's near accident and the plane episode to his father, who agreed that the whole affair was becoming dangerous. He advised the boys to be extremely alert and not to take any chances.

"There are dozens of planes of that make at the airfields near Bayport," Fenton Hardy pointed out. "On the other hand, it could have been flown in from some place else just for this job."

"That's right," Joe agreed. "The pilot might be

a lone wolf with a contract to knock off the *Flying Express.*"

"If so, that makes it all the worse. It means that the ringleader will stop at nothing. You'd better warn Given. Stay on guard and keep in touch!"

Joe reported the conversation to his brother.

"Mr. Given can expect trouble," Frank said. "Big trouble. And I don't need Chet's star charts to make that prophesy!"

Joe nodded. "Let's go talk to our client."

They found Given in the rear cabin. He complained that he would be ruined financially if the *Flying Express* suffered any more delays.

"Trouble!" he snorted derisively. "Of course I've got trouble! But there might be less of it if you two would show me some real detective work. And don't forget I have a return trip this evening! I expect you to do better on the way back to Bayport than you've done since we left it!"

"We'll be on the alert, Mr. Given," Frank assured him. "You can depend on it."

As the Hardys walked up the narrow steps to the apparently deserted stern deck, Joe said soberly, "We'll have to come up with something double-quick to show Given he didn't make a mistake by hiring us. But what?"

"Like stopping a fight!" Frank exclaimed. "Look!"

Near the stern railing two females were fighting like cats.

"Wow!" Joe exclaimed. "Rather unladylike! Let's break it up before one of them loses her hair!"

The two were wrestling along the rail, kicking and punching wildly. One was a blonde in a dark-green dress. The other was a rather heavy-set brunette in a light-blue dress torn in several places.

Suddenly the brunette struck a blow with her fist straight from the shoulder. The blonde took the full force of the punch, reeled backward, hit the rail, and flipped over into the water.

Frank and Joe grabbed her assailant. The torn dress shredded in their grasp. The black hair came loose and fell to the deck. The Hardys gaped.

Standing before them, blowing and wheezing, and nursing a skinned knuckle, stood Chet Morton!

CHAPTER V

The Mysterious Artist

CHET had a pained expression on his usually beaming countenance. He puffed like a porpoise, his torn dress revealing a checkered shirt and blue jeans. Between gasps he explained that he had come aboard the *Flying Express* in disguise to do some sleuthing of his own.

"But you were fighting with a lady, Chet," Joe protested indignantly.

"Lady! Are you kidding? That's the man we spotted coming out of the phone booth in Bayport. He wore a maroon dress before!"

"Ouch!" Joe exclaimed. "What numskulls we've been! Better start a rescue operation pronto!"

"Save your energy," Frank said. "It's too late." He pointed to the man in the water, who had no intention of being picked up by the hydrofoil. While his blond wig drifted away on the tide, he ripped off his dress and with vigorous strokes swam rapidly away from the hydrofoil.

"Expert at the Australian crawl," Frank commented. "But he'll have a problem making it from this distance."

"He won't have to," Joe said. "Look!"

A speedboat came racing over the wave tops. Its driver curved around in a circle of foaming white water and threw out a line. The swimmer climbed in and the boat made for shore.

The boys watched glumly.

"That boat must have been tailing us all along," Frank observed. "Maybe the skipper was watching the fight through binoculars."

"How did you latch on to our 'girl friend,' Chet?" Joe wanted to know.

"I drove into town this morning to get a prescription for my mother. Blondie was in the drugstore, asking for motion-sickness pills in her lovely deep voice. She mentioned the hydrofoil. So I thought it might be fun to tail the disguise in disguise."

Joe laughed. "Considering how little time you had, you did a good job on your outfit."

"I borrowed one of my mother's dresses and Iola's wig. They don't know it, though."

"Wait till your sister finds out. She won't like this!"

Frank picked up the disheveled hairpiece and handed it to Chet, who stuffed it inside his shirt.

Then he pulled off the tatters of his mother's dress and deposited the bundle of rags in the sea.

"We thought you had missed the boat," Frank said as the dress disappeared in the wake.

"No. As a matter of fact, I got here early. Spotted Blondie on board and tailed her. I lost her once, briefly, and then found her again leaving the stern in a hurry. I looked down and saw you riding the foil, Frank! So I yelled for help."

Frank whistled. "And Callie wanted to know if my female rescuer was pretty!"

The boys laughed.

"Let's go get some chow," Chet suggested. "That sea air and this nerve-racking detective work gave me an appetite!"

They met Iola and Callie in the lounge. While they were munching on sandwiches they had brought along, Chet explained his private sleuthing to the girls, leaving out the part of the disguise, however.

"Hey," Joe said after a while, "we're losing speed!"

The motors of the *Flying Express* diminished to a low purr and the hull sank gradually until it hit the water, moving forward in the manner of an ordinary boat.

Through the loudspeaker boomed the voice of the pilot: "Ladies and gentlemen, we are about to dock at Providence! Watch your step going ashore."

The Hardys and their friends filed onto the dock, and walked up into the quaint town with its gray-shingled houses. Souvenir shops and seafood restaurants lined the main street. Tourists milled around and mingled with the denizens of the Cape Cutlass artists' colony—good-looking girls in slacks with wind-blown hair and suntanned men wearing beards and sandals.

Callie and Iola were entranced by the artcraft shops. They dragged the boys into one after the other until Chet protested, "This hike is too much for me. You girls appear to be in training. Suppose you go it alone!"

Frank and Joe agreed. They were standing in front of a place called the Decor Shop, which specialized in feminine attire. Knickknacks filled the display window, along with carved driftwood and mannequins in colorful swimsuits, beachwear, and casual summer dresses.

"Okay, fellows." Iola said. "You disappear for a couple of hours while we look around."

"We'll meet you later at the Pizza Palace down the street," Callie added.

The boys moved off as the girls vanished into the Decor Shop.

"What shall we do now?" Joe asked.

Chet glanced at his watch. "I'm just about due at the Starfish Marina. How about coming with me? I'll introduce you to my new boss."

The owner of the marina was Al Hinkley, a

typical seafaring type, tanned from years of expo-
sure to wind and salt air, crinkle-eyed from hours
of gazing at distant horizons from ships beyond
sight of land. He gave the Hardys a friendly welcome, and said that Chet's job would be that of an
all-around assistant.

The youth would check the boats as they were
hired, keep them tanked up with gas, rent fishing
rods and nets, and service the skippers who
moored there.

"Quite a responsible position," Chet boasted to
his friends. "Hardly a sailor will be able to make
it out into the bay without my expertise!"

Al Hinkley corrected him mildly. "Not quite,
Chet. We have strong competition. Still, I do run
a profitable business here, and I want to stay in
business. So be careful about counting the boats
every day. I can't afford to lose any."

Frank and Joe strolled around the Starfish Marina and admired the boats at anchor.

Joe noticed a man about fifty yards away. He sat
at an easel, wielding a brush. But there was something odd about him. Each time a person walked
close enough to see his painting he quickly put a
blank canvas over it.

"Frank, look at that guy. Wonder why he's so
secretive?" Joe asked.

Frank observed the artist for a while and
shrugged. "Maybe he's shy."

"I'm going to take a stroll and check out his masterpiece if I can," Joe said.

When he approached, the man hurriedly picked up his blank canvas, placed it over the painting on the easel, and gave Joe an angry glare. Baffled, Joe walked back to the Starfish Marina.

"I know artists are supposed to be sensitive," he told his brother, "but this guy is a little too jumpy to be for real. I vote that we go all-out to see what his art work looks like."

Borrowing a pair of high-powered binoculars from Chet, who was now in charge of the marina, the Hardys found a vantage point behind a pile of fish nets, from where they had a clear view of the easel.

Joe focused on the painting, studied it, and handed the glasses to his brother. Frank peered through them.

"Why, it's a detailed drawing of the marina!" he exclaimed in astonishment. "From the jetty to the boats at anchor!"

"It's not a painting, it's a layout. And he's trying to conceal it," Joe summed it up. "Fishy?"

"Fishy. Let's talk to him."

Just then the man folded his easel, jammed it under his arm with his canvasses, jumped from the dock into a speedboat tied up there, and roared off.

"Too late!" Joe grumbled.

"It's a detailed drawing of the marina!"
Frank exclaimed

They went back to the boathouse. Chet listened to their story about the mysterious stranger, and promised to keep an eye on him if he should return to the area.

"Incidentally," Chet went on, "Mr. Hinkley is an interesting character. He's a Lion."

"So what? Dad's a Rotarian," Joe said.

"That's not what I mean. Mr. Hinkley was born under the sign of Leo. Trouble is, that makes him fire!"

Joe frowned. "Quit your doubletalk, Chet. Is that some more astrological lore?"

Chet stated authoritatively. "Each sign of the Zodiac is either earth, air, fire, or water. Mr. Hinkley is fire because he's Leonine. As a Cancerian, I'm water. Not a good combination! Water goes better with earth. Now if only he were earth! Between us we'd be growing a bumper crop of—"

"Grass!" Joe interjected.

"No siree, fat green dollar bills. One of us was born at the wrong time." Chet sighed mournfully. "Well, see you later."

He went off to take care of a customer, and the Hardys walked back into town for their appointed meeting with the girls. But Callie and Iola were not in the Pizza Palace.

"They must still be on their shopping spree," Frank complained. "Let's go back where we left them!"

The Decor Shop was closed when they got there.

"What now?" Joe inquired irritably. "Do we have to look all over Cape Cutlass for them?"

Frank peered through the window. Suddenly he started as if he could not believe his eyes. "The girls are inside!" he cried. "I can see them, but something's wrong! They're sitting on stools with their heads on a display case! I'd swear they're unconscious!"

The boys banged on the door and shouted. But the only response was the echo of their own voices. The figures did not move.

Thoroughly alarmed, Frank told Joe, "You stay here and do what you can! I'm going for the police."

He ran down the street, through the crowds that had dwindled with the closing of the shops. Music drifted out of the Pizza Palace. People were turning off the sidewalks into the restaurants for dinner.

At the end of the avenue Frank caught sight of a blue uniform. He ran to the policeman. "Officer, am I glad to see you!" he burst out. Quickly he explained what had happened—how the girls had failed to keep their rendezvous after shopping and how they were now locked in the Decor Shop.

"We'll see about this!" the policeman said, leading the way up the street on the run.

When they joined Joe at the Decor Shop, the police officer forced the door open.

The burglar alarm went off with a terrific racket, bringing a crowd of passers-by to the scene. They craned their necks for a view of the interior. More policemen came in a patrol car and cordoned off the area.

The Hardys took no notice of the turmoil. They hastened over to the motionless figures on the floor and halted dumbfounded.

They were mannequins—dummies wearing Callie's and Iola's jackets!

CHAPTER VI

Collision Course!

FRANK and Joe scurried through the Decor Shop in search of Callie and Iola. Frank peered under the counters, opened closets, and fingered his way along rows of dresses hanging on the racks. Joe took the office first, and then went into the storeroom, where he rummaged through crates and barrels.

Converging in the middle of the store once again, they shook their heads in distress. The policeman had been inspecting the doors and windows. There was no indication of forced entry.

"Hank," the officer called to one of the men from the patrol car, "let's get Mrs. Lane down here. She owns the place."

"Roger." Hank got into his car and drove off. About fifteen minutes later he was back with a gray-haired, middle-aged lady. She gasped in

47

amazement when she saw her mannequins in Callie's and Iola's jackets.

"Those dummies were in the window when I went home," she insisted. "I can't imagine why anyone would set up a fake scene like that. . . . The two girls? . . . No, I don't remember seeing them. But then I see so many girls during the day. I do hope nothing has happened to them!"

"Amen to that!" Frank said anxiously. "But we've got to find them pretty soon or else sound a general alarm that they've been kidnapped!"

While the policeman talked to Mrs. Lane, Joe took Frank aside.

"It's only an hour and a quarter until the *Flying Express* starts for Bayport. We've promised to be on board! What'll we do?"

Frank replied, "We can't go without Callie and Iola. Wait a minute! Mrs. Lane doesn't remember the girls. But maybe one of her employees does. Suppose we get on the phone and question all of them?"

They told their plan to the policeman. "Good thinking," he said. "You boys man the phones in the office while I make out my report."

Mrs. Lane supplied a list of her employees and the boys began dialing.

"Zero!" Joe reported, breaking the connection after his first call.

"Same here," his brother said disconsolately. "Let's hope we have better luck with the rest."

Thoroughly dejected, Joe reached the last name on his list. A part-time clerk answered.

"Yes," she replied to Joe's query. "I remember those two girls."

Beckoning Frank to listen in by way of the extension, Joe begged the clerk to go on.

"Not much to add," the voice said. "All I saw was that they were having a conversation with a man. Then the three of them left together."

"Who was he? Do you know his name?"

"Yes—Rance Nepo. He runs the photography store around the corner."

"Thank you," Joe said, and hung up. "There's our lead, Frank!" He grabbed the jackets, and together the boys ran to the photography store. It was a small place, with dust-covered cameras, rolls of film, and art books in the windows. As they entered, a warning bell jangled.

From the back room emerged a red-haired man with a stubble beard. "Are you Rance Nepo?" Frank asked.

The man cracked the knuckles of one hand in the palm of the other.

"Why, yes," he said. "Need some film?"

"No," Frank said and quickly introduced himself and Joe. Then he inquired about the girls. "We heard you talked with them and that they left with you," he said.

Nepo admitted that Callie and Iola had accompanied him out of the Decor Shop.

"Nothing wrong with that, was there?"

"Of course not, Mr. Nepo. But please try to remember. Perhaps the girls mentioned where they were going next?"

Nepo went on. "The blonde was interested in miniature flash bulbs. She'd just bought some kind of figurine decorated with them. I heard her ask where she could get more. The clerk said she had no idea, so I introduced myself and said I had that sort of information at my place."

"So they came here with you?" Frank asked, surprised.

"Yes. I let them look up the company in *Photographer's Guidebook*. When they found what they were looking for, they left. Said they were going to the Pizza Palace to meet a couple of fellows who would probably be late."

"Thanks. That's us!" Frank said.

Nepo snickered. "Good luck with the girls! I think you may need it!"

Frank and Joe thanked him and left. "Let's try the Pizza Palace again," Frank said tensely.

They entered and scanned the restaurant anxiously.

"There they are!" Joe said.

They found Callie and Iola seated at a table for four.

"Where have you two vagabonds been all this time?" Callie demanded irately.

"Don't you realize," Iola added, "that the *Flying Express* is leaving in a little while?"

"Wait a sec," Joe retorted. "Frank and I were here on time. You were nowhere on the horizon, so we went looking."

"Must have just missed you," Callie said, smiling.

"What worrywarts!" said Iola. She beckoned to a waiter, who instantly brought the pizzas pies they had ordered. Frank's and Joe's were loaded with pepperoni.

"Your reward," Callie teased.

Before they started to eat, Frank called the police and reported that the girls had turned up, then went back to the table.

"This hasn't been our day!" Iola said. "Our jackets were stolen while we were in the camera shop. I can't imagine—"

She broke off as Frank produced the two garments from behind his back. "How did you ever—?"

"We'll tell you later," Frank interrupted. "Let's get going or we'll miss the boat!"

Joe paid the check and they dashed through Providence to the dock.

The *Flying Express* was still there. Two minutes later she moved out into deep water, gathered speed, and gradually raised her hull into the air for the run back to Bayport.

Spencer Given approached Frank and Joe with a forlorn expression. "Notice anything different this trip?"

Frank looked around. "Obviously we don't have as many passengers."

"That's the point. A lot of people think that the *Flying Express* isn't safe. They've dropped us! They're traveling home to Bayport by bus. You understand what I'm up against."

"We understand, Mr. Given," said Joe. "We'll do our best to restore confidence in your commuter service."

"So will we," Callie said. "Iola and I would recommend the *Flying Express* to anybody!"

Given permitted himself a thin smile. "Thank you. We'll see how your boy friends do on the return trip."

The four settled down in the lounge and the Hardys told of their harrowing experience at the Decor Shop.

"So! You thought we were dummies!" Callie said. "Iola, I don't know how we should take that!"

"It's not funny," Frank said. "We thought you were hurt."

"We know," Iola said, and put her head on Joe's shoulder.

Frank asked, "Are you sure you didn't lose the jackets?"

"They were definitely stolen!" Callie declared.

"We had them when we went into Rance Nepo's shop. While we were getting the address of the flash-bulb company, they disappeared. We thought one of the customers had taken them."

"Or," Iola conjectured doubtfully, "it could have been Mr. Nepo. We didn't exactly keep him under surveillance while we were going through *Photographer's Guidebook*."

"You're right. We can't count out anyone at this point."

"The whole thing seems so childish," Iola said.

Frank shook his head. "I doubt that it was merely a prank," he said. "There's more behind it."

"It could be a warning of some kind," Joe said.

"Or else someone wanted to keep us here. Delay us enough so we'd miss the boat. Maybe some dirty work has been planned for this trip!"

The group fell silent, thinking it over, and Frank broke the spell.

"All we can do right now," he said, rising, "is circulate and keep a sharp eye on all the passengers."

"Let's separate," Callie suggested. "Iola and I'll go forward; you boys go aft."

They strolled around, casually pausing to chat with people. Frank and Joe passed the girls twice, but neither had anything to report.

Later Joe remarked to his brother, "We're almost at Bayport. Nothing has happened so far."

"Keep your fingers crossed!" Frank replied.

Dusk was beginning to fall as the *Flying Express* headed into Bayport Harbor. The lights of the city flickered in the distance and a rising moon cast silvery rays over the water. Small craft were converging on the docks from every point in Barmet Bay.

The pilot of the *Flying Express* cut his engines and the hydrofoil slowed for the approach to her berth, a few hundred yards off the bow.

People began to stir, collecting their belongings or simply waiting for the moment when the gangplank would be lowered.

The Hardys stood on deck, near the pilot and Spencer Given, watching the activities in the harbor. Through the dim light two powerboats, one behind the other, streaked in at right angles to the hydrofoil's course.

"I hope those guys have the common sense to change their course!" Joe muttered.

A moment later Frank yelled the warning:

"They're not veering off! They must be a couple of lunatics! Hold on tight. There's going to be a crack-up!"

It was too late for the pilot to do anything but watch in horrified incredulity. Given winced, and ducked as if he could not bear to see what was about to happen.

The first powerboat flashed across the bow of

the *Flying Express*, missing the bigger craft by a hair's-breadth, and vanished into the darkness of the bay.

The powerboat following behind never had a chance. As the hydrofoil plowed into it amidships there came the sickening sound of splintering wood!

CHAPTER VII

Diver's Peril

THE whistle aboard the *Flying Express* shrieked as the pilot threw the hydrofoil into reverse. Passengers screamed in fright and questions flew back and forth.

"How did it happen?"

"Was anybody killed?"

Frank and Joe did not wait for answers. Instead they raced for the life preservers hanging from the cabin walls and flung them into the bay.

After kicking off their shoes, they dived into the cold water.

The boys scanned the gloomy waters for the sight of a bobbing head. Nothing. Not even a piece of flotsam could be seen in the semidarkness.

"This job is too big for us!" Frank called to Joe. "They'll have to bring in the Coast Guard!"

By the time the Hardys had climbed back aboard, a message for help had been sent. Within half an hour two Coast Guard cutters converged on Barmet Bay. Their searchlights probed the misty darkness, illuminating the place where the powerboat had been hit. An officer directed the search from the pilot house of the *Flying Express*. He ordered his subordinates to scout the bay in a crisscross pattern.

The Hardys had worked with the Coast Guard on previous cases. They knew these professional sailors would find anything afloat. Their faith was soon rewarded.

"Debris here, sir," came a voice from the darkness. "The stern and part of the sides of the powerboat. Shall we tow it ashore?"

"Roger! We'll be coming right behind you for an inspection of the wreckage."

Spencer Given had been waiting, pacing up and down in despair. "Thank goodness for that order! My passengers are threatening to swim to shore if we keep sitting out here in the bay. I'm just thankful that the hydrofoil hasn't been ruined—only a dent in the bow that can be repaired. I wish my nerves could be repaired as easily!"

The Coast Guard officer nodded to the pilot, who started the motors again and brought the *Flying Express* slowly up to the dock. Ropes were cast onto the jetty and quickly secured around the metal bollards. The gangplank fell into place and the passengers streamed ashore, many of them grumbling that they were late for dinner.

Frank told the girls to drive home in the Hardys' car, while the boys went over to the Coast Guard office for the official examination of the debris.

The nose of the hydrofoil had caved in one side of the powerboat, and smashed through the opposite side. The stern had been twisted around and battered by the force of the collision.

"Any idea who she belonged to, Officer?" Joe inquired.

"No. And if this is all that's left, we may never find out. The impact of the hydrofoil ripped the license number off the powerboat!"

"What next?" Frank put in.

"The Bayport Police Department will have to send frogmen down to see what's on the bottom of the bay. If they find the motor, we may be able to fix the identity of the owner from the serial number."

"We're experienced scuba divers," Joe said quickly. "Perhaps we could help."

"Good thought. Get your gear and be here at six A.M. sharp!"

"Yes sir!"

The police launch was already revved up when Frank and Joe arrived the next morning. Two divers were testing their equipment; a third readied grappling hooks. Last-minute instructions were being given about the site and the mission. Then they pushed off into the bay.

"The water looks more friendly at sunrise than during the night," Frank commented.

Joe yawned. "Maybe it does, but somehow I don't feel my best this morning."

Frank laughed. "Come on, wake up. The bay is kind of deep at this spot, and we'll need all our energy to survey the bottom."

The boys peeled off their clothing down to their swim trunks, edged their feet into flippers, tested their aqualungs before pulling them on, and eased over the side into the bay along with three frogmen. Down they swam through the sunlit water to the murky depths.

As they drew within sight of the bottom, Joe dropped behind. He felt woozy. He was losing his ability to concentrate. A warm comfortable feeling swept over him.

Joe closed his eyes, stopped moving his hands and feet, and surrendered himself to the gentle movement of the current. Why was he down there? He couldn't remember and didn't care. All he wanted to do was to go off into a deep sleep.

Suddenly a hand jerked his arm violently. Frank was staring into his face.

"Good night!" Frank thought. "Rapture of the deep! Joe has nitrogen narcosis!"

He and Joe had read about nitrogen narcosis, one of the main hazards of skin divers going to great depths. This condition usually becomes evident below a hundred and thirty feet, but can also occur at lesser depths if a diver goes down at a time of low vitality.

Frank grabbed Joe's elbows from behind and gave a hard kick with his flippers. The two rose straight up through the water in a cloud of bubbles.

Joe's brain gradually cleared as they ascended. Realizing what had happened to him, a chill ran down his spine. When they cut the surface, Joe had command of himself again.

The boys clung to the side of the boat, breathing hard.

"Thanks for the assist," Joe gasped.

"Get into the boat," Frank ordered. "You've had enough."

Despite Joe's protests, he helped him into the launch, then dived again. Near the floor of the bay Frank spotted it. Half concealed in the mud lay the motor from the powerboat.

At Frank's signal the frogmen came swimming in. They put a cradle of rope around the motor, tugged on the line, and watched it move toward the surface. Then all the divers came up and boarded the launch.

"No serial number," Frank said in disgust after examining the engine. "It's been filed off!"

"Undoubtedly the powerboat was stolen," said the officer in charge. "Anyway, we've got the one piece of equipment we were looking for. Since we haven't spotted any bodies, we might as well return to port. The case belongs to the police chief from here on."

In his office at headquarters Chief Collig toyed with a pencil while Frank and Joe related all that had happened. He frowned.

"It's a real mystery," he said. "Have any ideas, boys?"

Frank spoke up. "I have a hunch that the powerboat was empty when the hydrofoil hit it."

"Empty, you say? Why do you think that?" Collig asked.

"Well, I think it was being towed by the other boat."

"Hum!" The chief nodded. "You mean the accident was planned?"

"It's entirely possible. That would explain why we didn't find any survivors of the crash. Nobody was in the water because nobody was in the boat."

Collig nodded soberly. "It's possible. Maybe you boys can bring in the proof. You've been involved in this case from the beginning."

"We'd be glad to help," Frank said.

"Good," Collig replied. "For starters, I'd like you to talk to the men who are opposed to Given's hydrofoil ferry. Pick up the *Bayport Times* at the street corner and you'll see what I mean!"

"Okay, Chief," Frank said as they left to buy the newspaper.

It carried a screaming headline: HYDROFOIL

SINKS POWERBOAT ON BARMET BAY. The subtitle read: NO SURVIVORS. The story said nothing about the smaller craft cutting across the bow of the *Flying Express,* which, the reporter hinted, had come barging into the harbor expecting every other vessel to get out of the way.

Enemies of the hydrofoil were quoted as calling it "a menace to the citizens of Bayport" and "a reckless venture that ought to be stopped." One man said bitterly, "We've already lost a power-boat. How many lives must be lost before we get rid of the hydrofoil?"

"Wow!" Joe commented. "They're really after Given's scalp. I feel sorry for him. This incident certainly wasn't his fault. Let's go talk to the group of small boat owners mentioned here. They're meeting at the yacht club right now."

The Hardys arrived at the club just in time to hear a speaker angrily denouncing the hydrofoil. "Here's the evidence!" he stormed, waving a newspaper. "The *Flying Express* must go!"

"To Cape Cutlass tomorrow morning!" Frank heckled from the rear of the hall.

"And back to Bayport!" Joe needled.

Heads turned and necks craned for a view of the individuals interrupting the proceedings.

"I don't know who these gentlemen are," the speaker snorted contemptuously, "but I imagine they're part owners of the *Flying Express!*"

"I wish we were!" Joe parried the accusation.

"We'd be pretty sure of a good return on our investment. The commuter service to Providence is going to be a success!"

"I hope they believe you!" Frank remarked under his breath. Aloud he said: "We're just a couple of passengers who happen to have been on board last night. We saw the accident. How many of you did?"

"He's right," a voice called out. "Charlie, were you there?" The speaker flushed and refused to answer.

Seizing the opportunity, Frank mounted the rostrum and explained the events of the previous night. "We suspect an arranged accident," he declared. "Somebody tried to put the *Flying Express* out of commission by towing that powerboat across its bow."

A murmur went through the audience.

"Certain groups fear the hydrofoil's competition and want it out of the way," Frank went on. "They're spreading rumors about its danger. Any idea who could be behind it?"

"Sounds as if you're accusing us!" one man said. "Sure, we don't like the hydrofoil but we're not criminals! No one here would sabotage her!"

A chorus of assent came from the rest of the audience.

"I'm sure of it," Frank told them. "But you sound as if you'd been sold a bill of goods concerning the hydrofoil. Why not give her proprietor a chance to prove that he won't interfere with any other boat on Barmet Bay?"

There were cries of "Fair enough!" and the meeting broke up.

Frank mopped his brow and joined his brother. "Think I convinced them?"

Joe nodded. "For the moment, anyway. But these guys could forget everything you said if any more incidents occur. Solve the case—that's the way to make them stay convinced."

The boys had scarcely reached home when the phone rang. Joe picked it up. "Chet's calling from Cape Cutlass," he said. "What's the matter, fellow? You sound as if some ill-starred disaster had struck."

"That's just it! Disaster beyond belief! I've lost my job! Somebody stole a cruiser from the Starfish Marina, so Mr. Hinkley fired me for negligence. What'll I do?"

"Hold on a minute," Joe said and briefed Frank. "You know," he told his brother, "it could have been stolen by the gang Dad's after. Maybe they're working their way north!"

"It's worth investigating," Frank agreed. "Tell Chet to stay put until we get there!"

Not long after the conversation, the Hardys were whizzing down the bay in their motorboat, the *Sleuth*. The trip to Providence was smooth, and Chet was waiting for them at the public dock.

The three held a council of war. If Frank and

Joe could find the missing cruiser, perhaps Chet would get his job back.

"We'll go see Mr. Hinkley," Frank said. "Want to come along?"

"Uh—no. I'll wait here. Pick me up later," Chet replied.

The Hardys guided the *Sleuth* to the Starfish Marina. Al Hinkley greeted them at the landing.

"Back again, eh?" he said. "Well, you won't find your pal here. He fell down on the job."

"We know," Frank said. Going straight to the point, he asked, "Mr. Hinkley, if we find your cruiser, will you rehire him?"

"Maybe," Hinkley hedged. "How do you expect to get my boat back?"

"We'll do some sleuthing around here," Joe explained. "No time left today, but we'll stay overnight."

"Hm!" Hinkley looked at them closely. "Go right ahead. That cruiser was very valuable. Tell you what. There's a cabin about a quarter of a mile from here. Look, you can see it."

He pointed and the Hardys took note of the place, which was little more than a fisherman's shack. "It belongs to a friend of mine who's out of town," Hinkley went on. "You can sleep there."

"Thanks," Frank said. "We'll make the cabin our headquarters."

They berthed the *Sleuth* and walked back to the jetty, where they briefed Chet.

"Gee. Thanks, fellows," he said.

"Want to stay with us in the cabin?" Frank asked.

"Sure," Chet replied.

On their way to the shack, a youth walked up to them. He was thin, lanky, and had sandy hair.

"Hi," he said. "My name's Skee. Say, are you interested in buying some marine equipment— secondhand and cheap?"

Frank and Joe exchanged glances.

"Why not?" Joe replied. "We could use a fog-horn for our cabin cruiser."

"Okay. What's your name?"

"Joe Hardy. When will you deliver the goods?"

"Soon."

"Well, how do we get in touch with you?" Chet inquired.

"Don't bother. I'll find you."

Skee ambled off in the gathering darkness and the boys proceeded to the cabin.

When Chet saw it he said, "This isn't the Cutlass Hilton."

"Forget it," Joe chided. "Didn't you think that Skee is a suspicious character?"

"No. Why?" Chet replied.

Before Joe had a chance to reply, Frank spoke up. "You think he's involved with the marina thieves Dad's after?"

"It's possible. That's why I ordered the foghorn. Maybe we can find out more about this stranger."

As Chet had said, the cabin was far from luxurious. It was small and dingy, but they were too tired from the day's events to care much. Flopping down on rickety cots, they were soon fast asleep.

When Frank awakened, the sun was already up. He stretched and was about to tumble out of bed when he heard a loud, grinding noise. It came from just outside the cabin. He roused Joe and Chet.

"Good grief, what's that?" Frank sprang up just as the side of the shack caved in with an ominous *whack*.

"Look out!" Joe yelled. "It's a bulldozer!"

CHAPTER VIII

An Unheeded Horoscope

FRANK pulled Chet from his cot, an instant before it was cut in half by the bulldozer's blade. All three dived out a window to safety.

The bulldozer's operator stared bug-eyed as his machine crunched to a halt.

"I'm sorry, boys. I had no idea anyone was inside." The operator said his job was to flatten the shack for a housing development.

"Who told you the cabin was empty?" Frank asked.

"The Fidelo Corporation. Did anyone know you were in here?"

"Al Hinkley from the Starfish Marina. He said we could use the place."

"Where can we find Mr. Fidelo?" Joe inquired.

"There's no Mr. Fidelo. That's just the name of the company."

"Who's the boss?"

"Big Malarky. He has an office in Providence."

The man waited until the boys retrieved their meager baggage before backing his machine for another thrust at the cottage.

Frank, Joe, and Chet hastened to the marina, where they talked to Al Hinkley. He shook his head in disbelief at their narrow escape.

"I heard yesterday that the building was due to be demolished," he admitted. "But no one told me they'd start so soon."

Convinced that there was nothing more to be learned from Hinkley, the boys left their suitcases at the marina and boarded the *Sleuth* for a reconnaissance expedition around the basin of the docks.

"The sooner we find the cruiser, the sooner our stargazer gets his job back," Frank said.

They had been searching along the coast for over an hour when Chet stood up and pointed toward the shore. "There's the boat!" he yelled.

The stolen craft was rocking in a swell, heading dangerously toward a rocky promontory.

"Full speed, Joe!" Frank ordered.

His brother headed the *Sleuth* toward the cruiser.

"Nobody's aboard! She's abandoned!" Chet cried as Joe pulled alongside. A quick inspection showed no damage had been done.

"What a load off my mind! Must have been

taken by some joy-riders who left it here after they'd had their fun!"

The cruiser was out of gas, so the boys towed it to the marina. Al Hinkley was as good as his word. Happy to have the missing boat back safe and sound he rehired Chet as his assistant.

As the Hardys helped Chet fuel the boat Frank spotted an outboard motorboat chugging back and forth in front of the marina.

"Recognize the fellow in it?" he asked Joe.

"Sure do. The artist who won't let anyone see his work. Wonder what he's doing out there. Want to go see?"

"Not yet. Chet can keep an eye on him. First we'd better visit Big Malarky. I'm still not convinced that the demolition business this morning was really an accident."

Joe nodded. "We'll see you later, Chet."

Frank and Joe found the office of the Fidelo Corporation. It was in the only high-rise building in Providence. A secretary ushered them into a room with oak paneling, a thick carpet on the floor, and a large kidney-shaped desk.

A big man sat behind it. He was at least six-three and two hundred fifty pounds, Frank thought.

Malarky got up. "What can I do for you?"

Frank told the story of their narrow escape.

"I'm awfully sorry," Malarky said. "Yes, I ordered the demolition. But I had no idea that the cabin was occupied."

Frank changed the subject. "You're in real estate, Mr. Malarky?"

"Right. We're developing a large area on the cape."

"Do you know Spencer Given?" Joe asked.

"Sure, sure. He's my only competition. One of us will do real well. Look here," he added abruptly, "I'd like to offer you my hospitality. I own a couple of cottages. One's empty, and no one'll knock it down, either!"

"Thanks, Mr. Malarky," Frank said. "We'd be happy to accept."

The builder handed him the key. "The cottage is close to the Starfish Marina, not far from the site of the wrecked cabin. Stay as long as you want."

As they emerged from the lobby a familiar face passed by in the crowd.

"Our mysterious friend the artist!" Joe hissed. "Let's trail him!"

The man led them down the main street to Rance Nepo's photography shop. He entered and spoke to the owner. The boys paused before the window but close enough to the open door to hear the conversation.

"I'd like to rent a camera for aerial photos," the artist said. "And I'll need some film."

Nepo replied, "I have an old Speed Graphic somewhere. Let me look in the storage room. I'll be right back."

Gesturing for Joe to follow, Frank walked into the shop. Close up the artist looked like a friendly individual—sandy hair, light-blue eyes, and a pleasant smile. He responded readily when Frank began to talk about photography.

Frank introduced himself and Joe. The stranger stuck out his hand. "Henry Chassen's the name. Profession: photography. Hobby: painting. Prospects: good, if I succeed on my present assignment, taking aerial pictures of Cape Cutlass, the kind that can be reproduced on post cards."

Frank and Joe exchanged glances. Was the stranger really as harmless as he sounded?

Frank was not convinced. He wanted to find out more about Chassen. An idea came to him. "Tell you what," he said to Chassen. "We're renting a plane for a spin this afternoon. Would you like to come along and take some pictures? We're licensed pilots."

Chassen jumped at the opportunity. "That'll be a big help. Save me a pilot's fee!"

"Okay. We'll meet at two o'clock at the Providence airport."

Just then Nepo walked in with a camera in his hand. He looked at the Hardys and grinned. "Did you find your girl friends?"

"Of course," Joe said breezily. "No sweat. So long, Chassen."

Frank and Joe had lunch before returning to the marina, where Chet was finishing a large pizza. They told him of their plan.

"Jumping Gemini, you can't do that!" Chet protested through a mouthful. "This is not the day for you to have anything to do with air travel!"

"Why not?" Joe demanded. "Is the sky about to fall?"

"Saturn has just moved out of Aries and—"

"Oh cut it out!" Frank sounded irritated. "The solar system can't be all that concerned about our doings here at Cape Cutlass. Saturn is millions of miles away. I doubt that it's going to interfere with one little airplane."

Chet shook his head sadly. "Mark my words, Saturn has set the stage for you today. There's no escape. Your trip will be ill-fated."

"We'll chance it," Joe said.

Leaving Chet to grumble about his disbelieving friends, the Hardys deposited their baggage at Malarky's borrowed cottage, then joined Chassen at the Providence airport, a short strip that handled nothing bigger than two-engine planes. They rented a four-seater model and took off with Frank at the controls.

As the plane zoomed over Cape Cutlass, Chassen snapped a series of photos.

"Good flying," Chassen complimented Frank. "I'm getting just the scenes I need."

After a while Joe remarked casually, "We saw you painting near the Starfish Marina. Something in oils?"

Chassen smiled. "Nothing but an outline for a picture to be filled in later. It's hard to work on the docks. People continually come up to see the picture. And I can't stand that."

"I see," Frank said. To himself he thought, "Seems we were on the wrong track to suspect this guy. He's on the level!"

"Could we fly along the coast?" Chassen asked. "I still need shots of the coves and inlets."

Frank complied. The plane passed over the indented coastline—flying and photography both going smoothly—until the engine began to sputter.

"Out of fuel!" Joe exploded, with a glance at the instrument panel.

Frank looked grim. He picked out a level stretch of shoreline and nosed down gradually. The wheels touched with a thump in the grip of wet sand, causing the aircraft to bounce wildly until it swerved around and came to a halt.

The three occupants were shaken but unharmed. They climbed out of the cockpit onto the sand and surveyed their situation. Frank noticed a stain on both sides of the fuselage where the fuel had been leaking out of the wing tanks. "Somebody sabotaged our plane!" he declared.

"Lucky for us this terrain was firm enough to land on," Chassen observed.

"Unlucky for us that we're so far from the nearest town," Joe replied.

Chassen shaded his eyes in the direction of the sea. "Say, isn't that a speedboat out there?" he asked.

"Sure thing!" Joe exclaimed. "They must have seen us land."

"They're coming to help," Frank said.

The boat beached itself and three men jumped out. They strode up the beach, smiling. They wore skivvies and dungarees, like fishermen out on a holiday.

"Perfect timing, gentlemen," Chassen saluted them. "We've had an accident. Could you help us get back to Providence?"

One of their rescuers made a quick move and the Hardys gasped.

They were staring into the muzzle of a revolver!

CHAPTER IX

A Buddy Lost

"OKAY, reach!" snarled the man with the gun. The smiles had vanished. "And no tricks!" His confederates frisked Frank, Joe, and Chassen.

"All clean, no rods on them," one reported.

"What's going on?" Frank demanded. "Is this a holdup?"

"They think they're on TV," Joe said.

"Real pop-offs, ain't you?" rasped the gunman. "How'd you like a taste of this?" He moved as if to pistol-whip Joe.

"Don't lose your cool, Spike!" the tallest man warned him. "We got nothing to gain from messing them up until later."

Frank, Joe, and Chassen were tied up, blindfolded, and carried aboard the speedboat, then it purred away from the shore.

Side by side on the floor of the cabin the trio discussed their predicament in low whispers.

76

"What are they going to do with us?" the photographer murmured.

Frank moved his wrists to get relief from the chafing caused by the rope. "Who are they? That's the question."

Joe shifted a cramped shoulder and managed a grin. "Our predicament lies squarely with Saturn!"

"How's that again?" Chassen asked.

"A friend of ours dabbles in the signs of the Zodiac," Frank said. "He warned us not to fly today."

"What are we going to do?" Chassen whimpered.

"Play it by ear, that's all we *can* do right now," Frank said.

After what seemed like a very long ride, two of the men removed the ropes and blindfolds and herded the captives on deck. It was growing dark. The speedboat pulled alongside a weather-beaten dock on the rocky coast.

"Out!" the leader commanded and pushed the boys toward a shabby boathouse.

Frank tried to get his bearings. High above the boathouse on the side that faced the road, he saw what seemed to be the glow of a red neon sign. The next instant he was shoved inside. The building was filled with dust and cobwebs. Joe started to sneeze.

"Okay, into the cabinet," ordered the leader,

and the boys were quickly marched toward a large closet.

The door swung shut with a clang. The lock grated into place. They were left in darkness. Moments later they heard the speedboat roar off.

"Not much air in here," Joe stated grimly as he felt his way around.

"We'd better get out quickly," Frank warned. "We'll suffocate if we don't!"

Henry Chassen was terrified. "You have any ideas?" he asked, his voice shaking.

"Not yet," Joe replied. "Let's find out what's in here besides us." He crouched down and began a minute examination of their prison with his hands. Frank followed his example.

"There's something under my heel," Chassen said. "Wait a minute— Oh, a book of matches!"

"Great," Frank said. "Light one, Henry!"

Chassen struck a match and held it up so that it threw a flickering light over the interior. Peering around, Frank and Joe spotted a pair of dirt-stained license plates nailed to the door.

"Real antiques," Joe remarked.

Frank read the year of issue on the plates. "Twenty years old."

True to their training in detection, the boys memorized the numbers on the plates.

"Ouch!" Chassen dropped the burnt match-stick as the flame licked his fingertips. Frank lit another one.

Chassen fumbled around the shelves lining the sides of the closet. "This might be useful," he suggested. "A blowtorch!"

"Nice going!" Joe said. "Here, let me see if I can cut through this door!"

He lit the torch, knelt down, and applied the blue flame to the area around the lock. Smoke rose from the heated metal.

Joe wiped the perspiration from his eyes and kept working. He was finding it difficult to breathe.

Frank's voice sounded far away. "Joe, I'm feeling faint! We're using up all of our oxygen! We may never get out alive! We'll—"

The two collapsed onto the floor of the cabinet —unconscious!

Later—how much time had elapsed they did not know—they regained their senses. Cold water was being splashed on their faces. A voice rang through the buzzing sound in their ears. "Fellows, are you all right? You had a close call!"

They opened their eyes to see Chassen bending over them. The door of the cabinet was open. They could breathe again!

Joe stood up rather shakily. "Henry, you're a lifesaver!"

Frank rose beside him. "Put it there, pal. We would have been goners if you hadn't got the door open. How did you do it?"

"It was taking too long to do anything with the

blowtorch, and I was feeling faint myself. So I ran my fingers around the edge of the door in a final attempt to get out—and presto! I tripped a catch at the top."

Frank patted him on the back. "We're out of the cabinet," he said, "but we're not out of the boathouse. Let's have a look at the doors!"

"Nuts!" Joe said. "They're locked."

"We might swim under them," Frank suggested. "I'll go first and see."

He lowered himself into the water, took a deep breath, and plunged straight down, feeling along the wooden door as he went. Finally he found the bottom and popped up on the other side of the barrier.

Everything was dark and silent. The surface broke again as Joe's head popped up beside him.

"One to go," Frank spluttered, "and we can all get away from here."

"Henry had better make it quick!" Joe said. "Here comes the speedboat! What'll we do, Frank?"

"We can't leave without Henry. Not after what he did for us. Wonder what's keeping him. He was supposed to come right after me."

"Probably couldn't make it under the doors. It's a tough swim for anyone. Look, we can't do him any good by staying here. Let's hide until the boat goes away and rescue him later."

Frank let himself quietly down in the water on

"We may never get out alive!" Frank said

the side of the dock away from the boat. Joe did the same. Only their fingertips and upturned faces showed, but the Hardys felt sure the darkness would complete their cover.

They listened. The motor was throttled back and the boat bumped the other side of the dock, sending ripples over the surface. Joe was taking in a breath when he shipped a mouthful of water.

He coughed and spluttered, breaking the tense silence like a cannon shot! Three men leaped from the boat and were on the Hardys like sharks. Two of them seized Joe, overpowered him, and hustled him into the boat.

Frank, threshing around in the water, felt a cold steel claw close over his wrist in a vicelike grip, and he, too, was hauled into the speedboat. As the claw released its grip on him, he collapsed beside Joe.

The boat sat dead in the water while the men debated their next move.

"We had three of them. Where's the third?"

"Guess he didn't make it out of the boathouse."

"That's fine. We can take care of him later."

"What do we do with the two birds we've got? The bottom of the bay is awful close, and it would solve the problem once and for all."

"That's not the way just now," said the man in charge. "There's a better way. Listen."

His voice sank to a whisper for a minute or two.

Then they started the boat and headed out. The leader spoke to the boys. They couldn't see his face in the darkness as he warned:

"We'll give you a chance this time, Hardys. But you're on notice that you've received your final warning. Keep your noses out of Cape Cutlass. Next time it'll be Davy Jones's locker for you!"

When the boat reached a point nearly out of sight of land, one of the thugs came back to the boys.

"On your feet, punks!" he growled. "Here, put these on!" He shoved a couple of life preservers around their waists, then each received a stiff push that sent him toppling into the water. The boat sped off into the darkness.

"No sense trying to swim," Frank said as he bobbed up and began to float. "We can't see the shore, and we might head for Europe!"

"Fortunately, it'll be light soon," Joe answered. "We should be able to get our bearings."

The rising sun began to light up the sea. Dimly at first, then more sharply, the contours of land began to take shape about two miles away.

"Cape Cutlass!" Joe could hardly believe it.

"More than that!" Frank shouted. "We're off the Starfish Marina!"

It looked like an easy swim. The boys removed their life preservers and headed toward shore.

As Joe started the crawl stroke he sighted something that chilled his blood—three fins cutting the surface of the water!

"Sharks!" he shouted.

Frank had already spotted them. He and Joe kicked furiously in a panic-stricken effort to ward off an attack by the tigers of the sea. This was one race they could not afford to lose!

CHAPTER X

Beware of the Claw!

ONE of the fish circled the two swimmers, cutting between them and the shore! Then it erupted from the surface and leaped high into the air. Sunlight glittered on the creature. It had a pointed snout with a mouth drawn up at the corners, as if smiling, and big round eyes.

Joe relaxed and grinned. "Hey, Frank. It's a porpoise!"

Frank brushed salt spray from his eyes. "Thank goodness!" He had just started to swim again when Joe called out:

"Look, there's a catamaran! Maybe we can thumb a ride."

The sailboat scudded before a strong breeze. The youth at the tiller brought her around to windward at a signal from his girl passenger, and came to a halt where the Hardys were bobbing in the waves.

"Ahoy there. Need help?"

85

"Sure do!" Frank shouted, and the girl tossed out a line.

The boys pulled themselves aboard the catamaran, and sprawled dripping on the deck.

"Thanks," Frank puffed.

"Don't mention it," the youth said. "I'm glad we sighted you. What happened?"

"We—er—were out in a speedboat and got dumped," Frank said.

The girl smiled. "We came out to watch the porpoise."

"Glad you did," Joe said.

"If you like," the boatman offered, "we can drop you off at the Starfish Marina. That's where we rented this catamaran."

"The assistant there is very amiable," the girl confided. "A little on the heavy side, but cute. He went out of his way to be helpful and had our boat ready in a jiffy."

Frank responded dryly, "Yes, we've met him. We've found him helpful, too!"

The sailboat deposited the Hardys at the dock, and then skimmed back out in search of the playful porpoise.

Chet Morton came running along the dock to meet them. He was accompanied by a man walking briskly behind him.

"Look! It's Dad!" Joe exclaimed.

Fenton Hardy grinned broadly as he greeted his sons.

Frank said, "We thought you were on Shark Island!"

"I was until Chet phoned home to say you were missing. Your mother passed the information on to me. She was greatly worried. So was I."

"We ran into a bit of trouble for a while," Frank admitted.

"But we've latched on to some good clues," Joe added.

They related all that had happened.

"We'll put out a missing-person report on Chassen," Mr. Hardy said. "Incidentally, the plane was found."

"Didn't I tell you trouble was coming?" Chet said. "Gosh, I'm sorry about Henry."

"I have some news, too," Mr. Hardy said. "Last week the maritime gang raided boats at Shark Island and picked them clean. I've got a list of what was stolen."

The detective pulled a notebook from his pocket and read off dozens of items. Suddenly Joe interrupted. "Dad, hold it! You just said foghorn. We ordered a foghorn from a guy who tried to peddle secondhand goods. He said his name was Skee."

Mr. Hardy nodded. "I suspected the thieves would peddle their merchandise all along the coast. Keep an eye out for that fellow. Perhaps you can learn who his associates are."

"Will do," Frank promised.

"Now tell me," his father went on, "what's the best clue to the kidnappers who seized you?"

"One of them grabbed me with a hook when I was in the water," Frank said.

"A hook?"

"That's right. It felt like a steel trap on my wrist."

Their father was silent for a few moments. "That sounds like Hooks Zigursky," he said. "If so, this whole affair is more sinister than I imagined!"

"Who's Hooks Zigursky?" Frank asked.

"One of the most dangerous criminals in this part of the country. He used to be a smuggler and bank robber. Had his hand blown off the last time he tried to crack a safe with a charge of nitroglycerine."

"What a pity," said Chet.

"Yes, a real tragedy," Mr. Hardy replied. "Brought on by himself. Since then he's worn a hook, a mechanical claw with which he has been known to throttle a man or beat him unconscious."

"Wow!" Joe exclaimed. "Now he's more dangerous than ever!"

"For another reason, too," Mr. Hardy said. "I was responsible for sending him to prison. The claw was the clue in that case also. Hooks received a stiff sentence, and he swore he'd be revenged on me someday. He served most of his time, and is out on parole now."

"I get it," Frank put in. "If he's up to some caper on Cape Cutlass and we're getting in his hair, he has two powerful motives to liquidate us. Interference and revenge!"

"But why didn't he kill us when he had the chance?" Joe mused.

"Maybe he'll watch us from now on, in the hope of locating Dad."

Mr. Hardy thought it likely and added, "I'd advise you to contact Mr. Given immediately. Warn him that thieves might attempt to steal fittings from the hydrofoil. There she is now, about to dock. Go ahead. I'll wait here."

The hydrofoil was on schedule. By the time the Hardys reached her, the passengers already had debarked. Frank and Joe noticed an acrid smell in the air, and saw Given pacing up and down, obviously agitated.

"Where have you been?" he stormed. "When I needed you most, you disappeared."

"What happened?" Frank asked.

"Arson. That's what! Somebody started a fire on the dock. Not bad, but enough to scare my passengers. It's out now." He pointed to some charred timbers.

"Sorry," Joe said. "We were unavoidably detained."

Frank warned him about the raiders, adding that he and Joe would ride the hydrofoil whenever they had time, which might not be often.

Given eyed them shrewdly. "Working on another case?"

Frank chose not to reply directly, saying only that they had an appointment to keep. They hastened back to Mr. Hardy, who stood alone on the marina wharf.

"Boys," he said, "I called Sam Radley and put him to work on the old license numbers you saw in the boathouse. He'll check them out. That way we may come up with a fix on the place where you were held."

Sam Radley was a skilled and highly dependable detective.

"We're going to work on it, too," Frank said. "We'll look for a red neon sign that throws a glow over the road behind the boathouse. I noticed it just before we were locked inside."

"That's a good idea. Meanwhile I'll get back to Shark Harbor to do some more investigating."

The boys went to the cottage to shower and put on dry clothes. After a quick breakfast they returned to the marina to ask Mr. Hinkley if he knew where they could rent a car. Both boys were surprised to see a familiar car pulling into the parking area. In it were Callie and Iola.

"So—the bad pennies have turned up once more," Callie said breezily as Frank and Joe greeted them with big smiles. "Actually we're relieved to see you. It's no fun wondering where in the world you are!"

"Tell us what happened," Iola said.

As Frank and Joe related the latest developments, Callie wrinkled her nose. "I think you're missing one of the most important clues. Why haven't you investigated the Decor Shop? I'd like to know who stole our jackets and set up those dummies."

"The Decor Shop?" Joe said. "Are you kidding? It's run by a sweet little old lady who couldn't possibly be implicated."

Frank looked reflective. "I think the girls have a point. Let's not jump to conclusions. I vote for a closer look at the Decor Shop."

"All right," Joe said. "But first things first. I think we should look for the neon sign before anything else."

"There's only one problem," Frank said. "We need transportation."

Callie grinned. "I know what you're getting at. Okay. Be my guest and use the car. We'll take the hydrofoil home."

"Thanks, Callie. You're a doll!"

An hour later Frank and Joe were driving down a dirt road thirty miles from the cape, the segment of the coast, as near as they could judge, where they had been held captive.

Frank broke the silence. "This could be just

about right. And look! There's a red neon sign with a boathouse behind it!"

In bold letters it advertised Calderon's Shore Restaurant. The place was nearly deserted.

Frank pulled off the road, parked in the shadow of some trees, and led the way past the neon sign to the boathouse behind the building. The doors were open, and a catwalk provided easy entrance.

"Wait a moment, Joe," Frank said. "It's pretty dark in here. There's a light switch near the door. Flick—"

His foot hit a net piled up on the floor and he stumbled into a pool of shallow water. Something nipped at his legs!

At the same time Joe said, "Hey, this isn't the right place." Then he burst out laughing. "Frank, you're in a lobster tank!"

CHAPTER XI

An Unequal Match

FRANK waded out of the tank, with lobsters clinging to the legs of his pants.

Joe laughed uproariously.

"Go ahead, make fun of me!" Frank said, shaking them off. "I'm lucky I escaped those crawly creatures alive!" Then he grinned. "I guess we had the wrong boathouse, all right."

Frank took off his shoes and poured water out of them. He set them aside while he removed his socks, then squeezed water from the bottom of his pants legs.

"Listen, Frank," Joe urged, "we'd better get out of here. If someone sees us, we might have trouble explaining why you went swimming with the lobsters."

"Right." Frank grabbed his shoes and they returned to Callie's car.

Next they scoured the shoreline farther down the coast. Spelling each other at the wheel, they passed several red neon signs and plenty of boathouses, but not one looked familiar.

"We certainly weren't this far down when we had our encounter with Zigurski!" Frank observed glumly. "We're nearly at Shark Harbor."

Joe agreed. "But since we've come this far, how about paying Dad a visit?"

"Good idea. It's only a short run to the bridge."

Fenton Hardy was staying at a small motel on Shark Island, a narrow spit of sand paralleling the mainland for about ten miles. He was not in his room. The desk clerk said he was at the State Police barracks nearby.

The boys found their father in the crime lab, where members of the felony squad were inspecting about fifty pieces of marine equipment. Mr. Hardy made the introductions.

"Quite a lot of goodies you collected," Joe remarked.

"But only a small part of what was stolen," a detective said. "This loot was found in an abandoned house."

Fenton Hardy pointed to a foghorn. "That will interest you."

Frank held it up. Someone had marked it in rough letters with the one-word notation: Hardy.

Joe exclaimed, "This must be the foghorn I ordered from Skee the other day!"

"Skee?" said another detective. "We know a Skee, too. Let's hear about yours first."

Frank described the youth who had offered to sell them used maritime equipment cheap. "Joe ordered a foghorn, and that's the last we've seen of Skee."

"Your description fits Skee very well," the detective stated. "He's the leader of a gang of young thieves who run in a wolf pack along the coast."

"Dad, that may be the cue for us!" Frank exclaimed. "Skee doesn't know we're on to him, and he'll probably turn up with another foghorn. As far as he knows, Joe is still his customer."

"If we nab him red-handed," Joe added, "we should be able to break up the wolf pack! And if by any chance Skee's tied in with that gang you're after, we may hit a double jackpot."

"And possibly find Henry Chassen," Frank said.

One of the policemen nodded. "That seems to be the ticket, Fenton. Your boys have developed a sound strategy. Attack the problem at both ends —Shark Harbor and Cape Cutlass—and see if the two lines of investigation converge on a single solution to all the robberies."

Frank and Joe drove back to Providence early the following morning, and went straight to the Starfish Marina. They found a mournful Chet Morton slumped in a beach chair. "Leaping Libra, fellows, am I in a jam this time!"

"What now?" Joe asked.

"A gang of hoodlums raided this place," Chet mumbled. "They boarded half a dozen boats, stripped them, and sped off before the police arrived.

"The Harbor Patrol says it will have a dickens of a job finding them," he added. "Too many coves and inlets along the coast where they could be hiding."

"Probably Skee and his boys!" Frank said.

"Just our luck," Joe complained. "We came back to Providence all primed to deal with this gang. But they pulled off the job while we were snoozing at Shark Harbor!"

"We've been outfoxed all right," Frank declared.

Chet's expression became even more forlorn. "You can say that again, Frank. They took the *Sleuth* with them, and a big rubber raft, too."

"What?" Joe blurted.

"The *Sleuth*'s gone," Chet said. "You must admit it's a prize."

"Joe, did you activate the electronic beeper as Dad suggested before we left Bayport?"

"Sure did. And the receiver's in my suitcase at the cottage."

"Good. Let's get it and drive along the shore. We might get a response from the *Sleuth*, and maybe even pinpoint Skee's hideout."

Twenty minutes later they were cruising

around Cape Cutlass, with Frank at the wheel, and Joe twisting the dials of the receiver in an effort to pick up a beep-beep.

"Hey, look," Frank said, gazing over the harbor. "There's something doing dockside. The *Flying Express* is surrounded by a flotilla of small boats!"

"Let's see what's up," Joe suggested.

Frank drove down to the wharf and parked the car. The two walked to the hydrofoil's berth, where some men were standing around arguing.

Joe elbowed his brother. "What do you know! There's our generous friend from the Fidelo Corporation!"

"It's Big Malarky all right," Frank replied. "He towers over everybody. Let's see what he has to say for himself."

In response to Frank's question, Malarky said, "Yes, I'll tell you. You've heard about the vigilantes of the Old West? They knew how to deal with horse thieves. Well, we're the aqualantes of Cape Cutlass, and we know how to deal with boat thieves!"

"But your flotilla doesn't seem to be chasing boat thieves," Joe commented mildly. "The skippers are circling the *Flying Express* as if they had nothing better to do."

Malarky's big face flushed. "Why would I want to do that?"

"I know why," piped a voice at the edge of the

crowd, and Spencer Given strode up to the builder. "You want to put me out of business, Malarky!"

The two men began a savage debate, full of mutual denunciations. A shoving match started.

"We'd better break this up!" Joe whispered. He stepped between the two men just as Big Malarky thrust a straight-arm at Given. Joe took the force of the blow, staggered, and fell to the ground.

Malarky helped him to his feet. "Sorry I hit you. I hope you're not hurt!"

"Not a bit," Joe replied sarcastically. "And I'll feel a lot better if you two will cut it out!"

"I've said all I had to say," growled Malarky, moving off with his men.

"I've got more to say," Given called after him, "and I'll say it next time I get the chance! Thanks for the assistance," he said to Joe. "I should have more sense than to get into a fight with that jerk. Well, see you later."

Frank and Joe ate lunch, then drove back to the road to continue their quest. It was evening and they were ready to give up the search as hopeless when suddenly—*beep-beep, beep-beep, beep-beep* came from the receiver of the electronic detector.

"We've located the *Sleuth!*" Joe exulted.

The sounds increased in intensity as they came

to the top of a steep cliff. The boys got out and peered down into the darkness.

"The *Sleuth* must be at the foot of this precipice," Joe said. "I'll get the flashlights."

"No, we can't use them. The gang may have left someone on guard. Better take him by surprise. I'll go first."

"Okay."

Frank eased himself over the edge, gripping the top of the cliff until he found a toehold on a protruding root and began the descent. Cautiously he put his foot on a jutting rock, tested it, and moved down to a sapling.

Frank's weight was too much. The small tree pulled loose and he plunged down the side of the cliff!

CHAPTER XII

Baiting a Trap

FRANK hit something soft, bounced into the air, and came down on his feet. His knees were bent and his hands extended, ready for an attack.

Nothing happened.

Then Joe called from the cliff. "Are you okay, Frank?"

"Yes. Get a flashlight."

The beam of the flashlight illuminated the base of the cliff, casting a soft glow on the *Sleuth*. A large yellow rubber raft lay upside down on the sand.

"I landed on the raft," Frank said. "Come on down, Joe, but watch yourself."

Quickly Joe found his way to the beach and doused his light. Together the boys put their shoulders against the bow of the *Sleuth* and began to push the craft back into the water.

Suddenly Frank stopped. "Listen. Someone's coming."

They ducked behind their boat and waited in the dim moonlight. A figure appeared, dragging something heavy across the sand.

Frank and Joe jumped up and shone the light in the stranger's face.

It was Skee.

"Hello," Joe saluted him nonchalantly. "Long time no see!"

The youth grinned weakly. "You scared me!" He set a power tool down and rubbed his hands. "I've been away for a while," he said. "Where've *you* been?"

"Oh, here and there," Joe replied airily.

Frank said, "Where's the foghorn you said you'd get us, secondhand and cheap?"

"Ain't got it yet." With a sidewise glance he added, "How'd you know where to find me?"

"Maybe Big Malarky's aqualantes told us," Frank replied.

Skee was poker-faced. "I don't know what you're talking about. Never heard of the outfit."

"How about this motorboat?" Joe inquired. "You own it?"

"Sure thing."

"Is it for sale?"

"Yeah."

"Well, we're on the lookout for this particular

model. But we don't want to buy a pig in a poke. Let's take it out for a trial spin on the bay, and if it runs smoothly, maybe we can arrange a deal."

"Are you crazy?" Skee protested sullenly. "Whoever heard of trying a boat at this time of night? It doesn't make sense!"

"Why not?" Frank retorted. "No time like the present. You've got something to sell, and we're out to buy."

"To tell the truth," Joe added slyly, "I'm not convinced this is much of a boat. Probably has a bad engine."

Skee took the bait. "Works like a charm. I'll show you!"

They pushed the *Sleuth* into the water and climbed aboard. Joe took the controls. Everything worked all right, so he upped the power and roared away from the shore.

"Let's see what she can do!" he sang out.

The boat responded to his touch like a spirited cow pony. It zoomed into a cove, turned broadside to the beach in a caldron of frothy water, and sped out. It skimmed nimbly among several small islands, slackened speed, went into reverse, and zipped forward again.

Skee was impressed. "You know how to handle this boat better than I thought."

"She's easy to handle!" Joe said. "I feel right at home behind the wheel!"

Realizing that Skee's attention was concentrated on the motorboat—which he hoped to sell for a good price—Joe maneuvered toward Cape Cutlass, and made a long curve right into the Starfish Marina.

Skee stood up in alarm. "What's going on? Oh no you don't!"

He plunged toward the side of the *Sleuth* in an attempt to jump clear, but Frank wrestled him to the bottom of the boat. They threshed around in a tangle of arms and legs.

Skee broke loose and leaped up to the jetty—almost right into the hands of Chet Morton.

"Get him, Chet!" Frank called.

A blow to the midsection and another to the chin decked the surprised Skee. Chet pulled the prisoner to his feet.

"Groovy!" Joe said admiringly and Frank put in a call to the State Police. A squad car came screeching to the scene and Skee was arrested, but he clammed up when questioned about his gang.

"He'll talk later," the trooper said and drove off.

"Good thing I was guarding the marina tonight," Chet said proudly. "How'd you like that belt to the breadbasket, Frank? Pow!"

"You did great, Chet."

The Hardys told what had happened and they all went to bed.

The next morning Chet had some time off, so

Frank and Joe took him down the coast in the *Sleuth* where they had left Callie's car.

"You can drive it back," Frank said, "while we scout around for some clues."

"Okay, fellows," Chet said.

First thing the Hardys did was to examine the power tool left by Skee. It was an electric grinding machine.

"I'll bet Skee was going to remove the *Sleuth*'s serial number," Joe deduced.

"Remember the motor we picked up from the bottom of the bay?" Frank said. "Its number had been filed off! Well, Skee won't have any further use for this tool. We'll take it back with us."

They put the grinder in the boat, and were about to shove off when someone shouted at them from the cliff top.

"Suffering swordfish!" Joe exclaimed. "Sounds like Henry Chassen!"

"It is!" Frank answered excitedly.

"Stay where you are, fellows!" the artist called. "I'll be right down!"

"What brings you here?" Joe asked him.

"I saw an abandoned car early this morning. But it's gone now. Where are you going?"

"To the marina."

"Take me along?"

"Hop in," Joe said, and they arrowed out to sea.

"Now tell us what happened to you," Frank said.

"To begin with," Chassen said, "I couldn't swim under those boathouse doors. So I went back inside and waited. Those three thugs returned, forced me into their boat, transported me out to sea, and pushed me overboard."

"Just what they did to us," Frank told him.

"I thought they were going to let me drown," Chassen went on, "but one of them threw a life preserver into the water. Except for that, I wouldn't be here. I drifted ashore ten miles south of Cape Cutlass. What an experience! I holed up for a couple of days just to rest!"

"You sure had us worried," Joe said. "We'll have to tell the police you're safe."

Chassen resumed his account. "After I reached shore, I heard that you both had landed from a catamaran at the Starfish Marina. I also heard that your father was there.

"I was hoping to meet him—I've never seen a famous private investigator in the flesh," Chassen went on. "It would be quite a thrill to meet the great Fenton Hardy. Where is he now? Providence, I hope."

"Sorry to disappoint you," Joe said, maneuvering the motorboat to the dock. "Dad's down at Shark Harbor."

"I'll take a raincheck. You must introduce me

sometime. So much for now. I'm off to the Decor Shop. The owner has commissioned me to do some paintings. She thinks they'll sell very well. Hope to see you soon. So long."

Chassen strode up the street.

Frank looked at his brother reprovingly. "Joe, you shouldn't have let on where Dad is!"

"Why not? Don't we agree that Henry Chassen is as honest as the day is long?"

"Maybe so. But suppose he tells somebody else, who tells somebody else—until half of Cape Cutlass has a book on Dad's activities."

"Sorry," Joe said soberly. "I should have been more careful."

Frank picked the electric grinder up and turned it over. "Here's the name of the hardware store it came from. Address on Main Street. This is one clue we can deal with in a few minutes."

"Right. Let's go there now."

The clerk at the hardware store examined the tool and then ran a finger down his register. "We sold this to the Atlas Garage. It's on the corner of Bayshore and Halibut."

The Atlas Garage was a large and busy place. One car stood on treads over the grease pit. Several others had been dismantled and mechanics were working on them. Two cars were being tanked up with gas.

Frank and Joe headed for the manager's office, where they explained that they wanted to inquire about an electric grinder purchased recently at the hardware store.

The manager ceased pretending to smile and became surly. "I'm too busy for questions like that!"

"But can't you simply tell us what happened to the grinder?" Frank asked.

"How should I know? Now get going!"

Joe grimaced as they left. "Boy, he's not out to win friends!"

"Well, maybe he really didn't know," Frank said. "But this needs further investigation. What say we come back tonight and look the place over?"

Joe grinned. "And what'll we do meanwhile?"

"We promised Callie to check out the Decor Shop."

"Okay, let's pay a visit there."

The girl at the gift counter was free. She readily answered the questions put to her by Frank and Joe. Mrs. Lane, the store's owner, was a pillar of local society and had a spotless reputation.

"What about Rance Nepo?" Joe queried. "He comes in here."

"Why not? He's a customer."

"Then there's Henry Chassen the artist," Frank said. "Can you tell us anything about him?"

"Mrs. Lane likes him, and likes his work. But then, we all do. We're glad she's buying some of his paintings."

The girl turned to an impatient customer. Frank and Joe went back to the cottage to await the zero hour of their next venture.

Midnight found them at the Atlas Garage.

"Kind of spooky!" Joe said in an undertone.

They sneaked around to the back, found an unlocked window, pushed it up, eased over the sill, and dropped into the interior.

"Forget the cars," Frank advised as he snapped on his flashlight. "Just look at the rest of the stuff."

The light flickered through the darkness and picked out a row of engines in one corner.

"Outboard motors!" Joe whispered hoarsely.

"What could be the reason—?"

Suddenly the room seemed to be flooded with stars. Frank and Joe slumped to the floor, knocked out!

CHAPTER XIII

Disappearing Act

THE split image in Frank's brain finally converged, and the blur changed to a vision of a plush office. Joe, sprawled beside him on a sofa, also was regaining consciousness.

Frank blinked at the oak-paneled walls and deep-piled carpet underfoot. Across from them, behind a kidney-shaped desk, sat Big Malarky.

Joe immediately became fully alert. He glanced at Frank and then at the building tycoon.

"Wh-what happened?" he asked, gingerly touching the back of his head.

"You were kayoed by a couple of my aqualantes. They spotted you prowling around the Atlas Garage at midnight, kept you under surveillance—then bingo!"

Frank shook his head sadly. "What a deal! We were there because we had traced the boat thieves to one of their hideouts!"

Malarky's eyes narrowed. "Do you have proof?"

109

"Sure!" Frank replied. "We saw several outboard motors in the back of the garage!"

Malarky was impressed. "I tell you what," he offered. "I'll have the local constable meet you there. We'll get to the bottom of this!"

Malarky picked up the phone and put in a call to the constable's office. "All set," he declared finally. "He'll be waiting for you."

The constable met the Hardys at the front of the garage. He took them directly to the office of the manager, who also had been called in.

"I have nothing against you taking a look around, Constable," the manager said. "These guys were making a nuisance of themselves yesterday, but now that it's official, go ahead."

The boys hastened to the back room with the constable.

Without even looking, Joe pointed to the corner. "There!" he blurted.

The constable scratched his head. "Where?"

Frank groaned. "Joe! The corner's empty! The outboard motors have been removed!"

"If you weren't Fenton Hardy's sons," the constable snapped, "I'd suspect some sort of game. As it is, I'll say you made a mistake, and let it go at that!"

Much depressed, Frank and Joe returned to the cottage, where Chet greeted them.

"What's the matter?" he asked. "You don't look too happy."

"Someone threw us a curve," Frank said morosely.

"And I suspect Big Malarky," Joe declared. He told Chet what had happened.

"That figures," Chet replied. "I've checked up on Big Malarky's birthday. Found it in the annual listing of the leading citizens of Cape Cutlass."

"What is he?" Frank inquired.

"Virgo! Governed by Mercury, and Mercury rules the hands. So I'd keep an eye on what Malarky does with his hands."

Joe nodded. "We'll have to be extra careful from now on. The crooks know we got close to them this time. They could decide to give us a one-way cruise next time. Maybe they'll come swarming through the windows tonight!"

"No problem," Chet argued. "We can rig up an early-warning system. You brought your bug, didn't you, Frank?"

"Sure thing." Frank went to his suitcase and removed a kit. Then the three hastened to the marina dock. After planting a detection microphone under a fish net, they strung a wire back to the cottage, through a window to a nightstand between the beds, where they placed the receiver.

Chet inspected the device with satisfaction. "There! Nothing can move outside without us being cued in electronically. Safe as a good horoscope!"

There were no visitors before bedtime, but

when the boys were sound asleep, the receiver began to crackle ominously.

Frank snapped wide awake. "Joe! Chet! Something's cooking at the dock." They dressed hurriedly, crept out the back door, and edged silently through the darkness toward the microphone.

Suddenly a *quack* broke the silence. There was a rustling of feathers, followed by splashing.

"A duck!" Chet exclaimed in disgust. "That's what brought us out at this time of night." He shook his head and the boys returned to the cottage.

The next morning Frank and Joe hastened over to the hydrofoil's berth. Spencer Given looked upset.

"He had less sleep than we did," Joe thought.

"I've got a court order," Given announced, "to keep those aqualantes away from the *Flying Express*. But Marlarky hasn't stopped hounding me. My plans for a real-estate development on Cape Cutlass are going up in smoke. People are turning down my discount offers on lots. They're afraid to buy at any price!"

"Why is that?" Joe asked.

Given waved a Bayport newspaper at them. "Here, read this!"

An advertisement had been placed by Big Malarky. It read: "Come to Cape Cutlass in safety by car, train or bus. What good is a discount if you don't live to enjoy it?"

"A duck!" Chet exclaimed in disgust

Joe folded the paper and handed it back. "Rather unethical, Mr. Given, but I'm afraid it isn't illegal."

"Not illegal," Given retorted testily, "but it's a threat, wouldn't you say?"

"No doubt about that," Frank agreed. "Malarky intends to run you out of business. We'll do our best to prevent him from doing it."

"Your best is what I'll need! Keep trying!"

The Hardys discussed what to do next.

"Let's talk to Henry Chassen again," Frank suggested. "Maybe there's something—some kind of clue—he forgot to tell us when he described his rescue yesterday."

"You know, we never even asked him where he lives," Joe reminded his brother.

"You're right. Maybe we can find out from the Decor Shop."

When Frank and Joe arrived there, Chassen and Rance Nepo were standing in front of the door talking.

"Hi, fellows," Henry said. "Rance is trying to sell me another camera."

Nepo smiled cordially and extended one of his instant models on the palm of his hand. "Here's a beautiful example of the art. Have a look through the range finder."

Frank raised the camera and began to take some practice views while Joe struck up a conversation with Nepo and Chassen. They spoke about the technique whereby a snapshot could be taken and developed almost immediately.

"We've come a long way in photography," Nepo remarked. "No more need to take pictures outside and develop them in a darkroom."

There was something about Nepo that made Frank uneasy, something he could not quite put his finger on. "How about letting me work this lovely gadget myself," he said. "Suppose I take a snapshot of you two."

"By all means," Nepo invited him. He was eager to show off this new and expensive model he had just received from the manufacturer.

Frank took a picture of Nepo and Chassen standing together. Sixty seconds later he removed a clear picture of the two men and held it up for inspection.

Nepo grinned. "Ever see a clearer photo?"

"Can't say I have," Frank admitted. He handed the camera back. While the other three were deep in the technicalities of photography, he pocketed the picture.

"Incidentally, fellows," Chassen said, "have you any pictures of your family? It would be interesting to see your parents together."

"The only one I happen to have is of Dad," Joe answered. He reached into his pocket for the passport picture of Fenton Hardy that he had picked up in Bayport and forgotten to give to his father.

Frank nudged him. "Wait a minute, Joe. You gave it to me. Here it is."

He brought out Sam Radley's passport photo and showed it to Nepo and Chassen. They scrutinized it intently before handing it back. "Looks like a man of action," Nepo commented. "Well, I'll have to go now. See you later." With that he left.

Frank and Joe questioned Henry again about his escape, but Chassen could shed no more light on their captors. He told the boys that he lived in a boarding house on Maple Street, then said good-by.

Joe was mystified on the walk back to the cottage. "Frank, why the exchange of the photos of Dad and Sam Radley?"

"I'm suspicious of Nepo. I don't want him to be able to identify Dad."

"Why do you suspect Nepo?"

"I'm not sure."

At the cottage Frank brought out the instant photo, placed it flat on the table, and studied it carefully. Joe and Chet looked over his shoulder.

"Somehow—somehow this guy looks familiar," Chet mused. Suddenly he exclaimed, "I've got it. Frank, quick, give me a pen!"

Frank handed him one and Chet went to work on the figure of Rance Nepo. With a few skillful strokes he put a fluff of curls around the head and sketched a flouncy dress.

Joe watched, fascinated. "What in the world are you doing, Chet?"

"Don't you see? This is the lady in the case. The one who phoned you in Bayport and knocked Frank off the hydrofoil catwalk!"

Frank whistled softly. "Of course! Rance Nepo is our phony blonde!"

CHAPTER XIV

Anchors Aweigh!

"Chet, you're a genius," Joe said. "You've got a great memory!"

Chet bowed modestly. "Thanks for the compliment. But after all, I had one advantage, Joe. I'm the only one who saw Nepo close up in his disguise. Shall we report him to the police?"

"No, not yet," Frank said. "Nepo thinks he has us fooled, which gives us a chance to fool him. Joe and I'll visit his shop tomorrow, and add a few loaded questions to the chatter about cameras."

Nepo's place was shut tight when they got there. A heavy green shade covered the glass panel of the front door and a large sign dangled by a wire cord. It said: *Closed—On Vacation*.

"Strange, he didn't say anything to us about taking off," Joe remarked.

"Not so strange, Joe, if he's up to something.

But Henry Chassen might be able to tell us what's cooking."

Chassen was not in his room at the boarding house nor at the Decor Shop. No member of the staff had seen him since the previous day.

"Did he say he was going on vacation with Rance Nepo?" Joe inquired.

The clerks said No.

"Something's fishy," Frank said gravely as they paused at the curb.

"We ought to warn Henry about Nepo," said Joe. "If he's traveling with Nepo, he should know that his companion doesn't wear a white hat. Let's tell the police now."

Frank shook his head. "There's no proof that Nepo's committed a crime," he pointed out. "We need solid evidence before we can go to the police."

Back at the Starfish Marina, the young sleuths found Chet in a tizzy again, and Al Hinkley hopping mad.

"More thievery!" the man fumed. "They came in here and lifted the outboard motors from a couple of my boats." He stalked off muttering to himself.

"I'm as burned up as Mr. Hinkley," Chet mumbled fretfully. "I hardly turned my back before the motors were gone."

"They just didn't fly away," Joe said. "Didn't you see anybody snooping around?"

"Not a soul."

"Don't throw in the sponge, Chet," Frank said. "Joe and I'll cruise around for a look-see."

Chet still seemed depressed. "Being a Cancerian," he said, "I'm bound to have some bad luck now. It's nice to have an Arian and Scorpion on my side. You're in the right House of the Zodiac this month to make discoveries and uncover plots."

"I hope so!" Frank said as the *Sleuth* churned out into the bay. Joe handled the controls. Frank sat at the bow, scouting the area around the Starfish Marina through high-powered binoculars.

He sighted a rowboat with two men holding fishing rods over the side. There wasn't another boat within half a mile, so Frank watched them for a few minutes.

"Slow down, Joe. I want a better look at those fishermen. They haven't moved their lines at all. See for yourself."

The *Sleuth* slowed to quarter speed. Joe locked the controls and joined Frank in the bow. Taking the binoculars, he surveyed the rowboat from stem to stern.

The two men hastily pulled in their lines, tossed them under a seat, unlimbered the oars, and began to row shoreward.

Frank took the binoculars. "They're going awfully slow," he said in a perplexed tone. "That rowboat can't be all that heavy. It's as if they were trailing an anchor."

Joe exclaimed, "Frank, you've hit on the answer! They're dragging stolen motors. I'll bet my sweet *Scorpion!*"

Joe went back to the controls and guided the *Sleuth* in the direction of the rowboat. As they drew closer, he asked Frank to take over. Then he skinned down to his shorts, lowered himself into the water, gave a hard kick, and arched below the surface in a long underwater dive that brought him beneath the rowboat.

He saw two chains extending down from the sides. Following one chain hand over hand, he reached the end—where an outboard motor was tied!

Joe's breath was giving out! His heart pounded, and there was a buzzing in his ears! He needed air!

Summoning all his remaining strength, he tugged hard on the chain and zoomed to the surface.

Gulping in air, he surveyed the scene. The rowboat had capsized and its occupants were floundering in the water.

"Help!" one of them shouted. "Help! Save us!"

Joe quickly swam over to one of the men, got a lifeguard's grip on him with an elbow under his chin, and boosted him up into the *Sleuth*. Frank leaned over the side, grasped the hand of the other man, and pulled him in.

Both collapsed in bedraggled heaps. Frank quickly bound their wrists.

"Let's not forget the motors," Frank said. "They're what we came here to get."

Joe got out a towrope, swam back to the overturned rowboat, fastened one end of the rope to a ring at its bow, and swam back.

Frank had the *Sleuth* moving as Joe climbed in. The rope tightened, and the motorboat moved toward the dock with the rowboat in tow.

Pulling into the Starfish Marina, Frank shouted to Al Hinkley, "Call the police! We've found your stolen motors."

Chet came running up. His round face broke into a big grin as Frank and Joe hauled the motors up onto the wharf.

"Well, that gets me off the hook, doesn't it, Mr. Hinkley?" he said as his boss emerged from the office after phoning the police.

"It does, as far as I'm concerned, Chet. But you'd better apply some elbow grease to those two motors. They need a lot of work after their dunking in the bay!"

The men from the rowboat were back on their feet by the time a squad car rolled into the Starfish Marina. Frank and Joe went along to headquarters to make a statement about the theft and recovery of the two outboard motors.

The prisoners were given dry clothing and then brought in for questioning. They were advised of their rights to legal counsel, then the police sergeant asked the first man:

"What's your name?"

"Eric Anderson."

"Where do you live?"

"No place in particular. I work at odd jobs wherever I happen to be."

The police sergeant turned to the second man, who said his name was Robert Meyer. He, too, had no steady job.

"You're both drifters?"

"Yeah. And we ain't talking."

Anderson shifted in his chair. "Give us a break, will you?" he whined. "The boss will drown us if we spill the beans!"

Frank poured a glass of water and held it out to him. As he started to drink, Frank fired a question.

"Is your boss Hooks Zigurski?"

Anderson choked over the water he was drinking. Sputtering and coughing, he reached for his handkerchief, blew his nose, and regained his breath.

"Never you mind who our boss is!" he growled. "Look. I want a lawyer."

"Okay," the sergeant said. "Book them for being in possession of stolen goods and supply counsel."

"I guess there's nothing more we can do here," Frank remarked. They set off for the cottage, where Chet was waiting for them.

Much to their surprise, so was Fenton Hardy!

"Hi, Dad!" Joe said. "Short time no see."

"What's up?" Frank asked.

The private investigator looked grim. He went right to the point.

"Boys," he said huskily, "Sam Radley has disappeared!"

CHAPTER XV

Under the Bed!

Sam Radley missing! Frank and Joe exchanged startled glances.

"We thought he was checking those license plates we saw in the boathouse," said Frank.

"He was," Fenton Hardy answered. "In fact, he reported back that he was on to something that would interest all of us."

"Maybe Sam found out who owned the plates!" Joe said excitedly.

His father nodded. "That's possible. Trouble is, he never passed the information on to me."

"Tell us what happened, Dad," Frank urged.

"Not much to tell. We were supposed to meet at Shark Harbor. Sam's car turned up in the parking lot near where I'm staying. The attendant remembers seeing him park. After that—no sign of Sam!"

Frank was about to speak when Chet interrupted. "Leaping Libra! What sign of the Zodiac was Sam Radley born under?"

Joe turned to him in annoyance. "What difference does that make? We're not reading horoscopes now. We're dealing with a man who's disappeared under mysterious circumstances!"

"Mysteries are my specialty," Chet responded. "When was Sam Radley born?"

Frank said resignedly, "We might as well get it over with. Sam was born in early December."

"Then he's a Sagittarian—the sign of the Archer. They are generally smart cookies. But the planets are out of kilter for them this month!"

Chet produced a small book from his pocket, flipped the pages to the sign of the Archer, and read in a booming voice, " 'This is a time of suffering from a big mistake. Retaliation is due.' "

"That's not too far off," Frank commented. Quickly he told his father about Rance Nepo being "the lady" in the case. "I made a mistake when I showed Sam's picture to Nepo. And Nepo captured Sam by mistake, thinking he was you, Dad."

Chet looked at him with an air of authority. "Well, whoever did it is in for big trouble this month. The book says retaliation. He'll pay for kidnapping Sam."

Fenton Hardy nodded. "The question is, Who does Nepo work for? Obviously he's connected with the gang trying to sabotage the hydrofoil.

But they'd hardly be interested in Radley. Nor in me, since I'm not working on the Given case. My only enemy at large now is Zigurski. He swore he'd get revenge when I sent him up the river. Perhaps he grabbed Sam to get back at me!"

Chet cleared his throat. "Mr. Hardy, Hooks Zigurski can't be the guy who grabbed Sam Radley!"

"Oh no? Why not?"

"Because Zigurski isn't near Shark Harbor! He's in Miami, Florida!"

"And how did you come by that vital piece of information?"

Chet looked apologetic. "I didn't mean to step out of line, Mr. Hardy. But I needed to know Zigurski's birthday to figure out what he's up to. So I used you as a reference with the State Parole Board. They told me Zigurski is in Florida. I hope you're not mad at me."

Fenton Hardy chuckled. "It's hard for anyone to get mad at you, Chet. What did the parole people tell you about Zigurski?"

"They said he was born on July twentieth. That makes him a Cancerian. The sign of the Crab."

Frank grinned. "That puts you and Hooks under the same sign, Chet! Makes you two of a kind, doesn't it?"

"Not at all, Frank. Zigurski was born on the cusp!"

"The cusp?"

"That means three days before or after the last day of a sign of the Zodiac. People born on the cusp have the characteristics of both signs."

"Such as?"

"Such as Hooks Zigurski. He was born between Cancer and Leo. He may look like a Cancerian on the outside, but he's Leo inside. I'm sure of that!"

"Is that good or bad?" Frank wanted to know.

"Bad news, in this case. A Leo likes to give orders. He has a habit of taking what he wants. Isn't that how you read Zigurski, Mr. Hardy?"

"Right on the button, Chet. If Zigurski is in Florida, he must have delegated the job of kidnapping me to someone else. He himself knows me and wouldn't have made the mistake of capturing Sam."

"Which brings us back to Nepo," Frank concluded.

"Right."

"I wonder why Hooks went to Florida in the first place," Joe mused.

"Could be to establish an alibi," Frank suggested.

Fenton Hardy nodded. "Yes it could," he agreed.

"If we only knew what caper he's planning now!"

Joe sounded desperate. "He might be tied in

with the boat thieves and the attempt to sabotage the hydrofoil! How can we stop him, Dad?"

"It won't be easy. But for a start, alert all the Cape Cutlass marinas. They're sitting ducks right now. But if we're lucky, the gang may be caught in the act!"

The detective got up from his chair and peered out the window. "I came up here secretly to give you the news about Sam Radley. Now I'd better get back to Shark Harbor and see if I can pick up his trail."

"How do we fit in, Dad?" Joe asked.

"Up here, you can watch out for Nepo and Zigurski. Either of them could be the key to this puzzle."

Suddenly Frank put his finger to his lips. "Sh! Listen! A prowler!"

Someone was moving around outside the cottage. Footsteps sounded softly as if the person was trying to avoid detection.

Fenton Hardy whispered, "I can't let anyone see me here. I'll hide under the bed." He got down on the floor and squirmed out of sight.

Frank stepped quietly to the door and jerked it open. A bent figure stumbled into the room.

"Mr. Malarky!" Joe exclaimed as the big man caught his balance.

"What a nice surprise," Frank added with a smile. "We'd like you to meet Chet Morton."

They shook hands and Frank went on, "We thought you had forgotten about us using your cottage. So you remembered after all!"

Big Malarky was embarrassed. "I nearly did forget you," he confessed. "When my secretary reminded me you boys were here, I came over to see if you were comfortable." With a sly grin he added, "See any more outboard motors?"

The Hardys laughed and Joe said, "Guess we all can make a mistake, Mr. Malarky."

Frank assured him that everything about the cottage was just fine. There was a bit more small talk about boating and then Malarky left.

"That's a Virgo for you," Chet observed. "Passion for details."

"Think Malarky's on the up-and-up, Dad?" Joe queried as his father crawled out from under the bed.

Mr. Hardy brushed his palms across the knees of his trousers, and straightened up. "I'm not too sure. He certainly sounded like a prowler. On the other hand, this is his cottage and you fellows are his guests. He had a plausible enough reason to be down here."

"I still suspect him," Joe asserted. "He may be a Virgo with a passion for details, as Chet says. But we know him as a tough operator who doesn't like competition. He's practically admitted that he's out to ruin Spencer Given and destroy the hydrofoil."

"I agree," Frank said. "Why should Big Malarky be concerned about our comfort? It's just as likely that he was snooping around for information about our connection with the *Flying Express!*"

"I'll leave that point to you," Fenton Hardy told them, "and take off while the coast is clear."

He opened the back door, took a look around to be sure no one was lurking near the house, and quickly slipped out.

The boys turned in early, and were fast asleep when their alarm system came to life. Frank was the first to hear it.

He shook Joe and Chet, and the three gathered around the receiver.

"No ducks this time," Chet murmured. "Men are out there on the dock."

"Let's listen," Joe advised in an undertone. "Maybe they'll give themselves away if we don't go barging in on their summit conference."

Several voices came through at once until one, who seemed to be the leader, called for silence.

"Get the boats going!" he ordered.

"What about the *Flying Express?*" another voice demanded. "Isn't that caper still on?"

There was a scuffling noise as if the speaker was being roughed up.

"You fool!" the leader raged. "Mention that again and you'll end up keeping company with the flounders!"

"Okay, okay! Leave me alone! It was only a slip of the tongue! Won't happen again!"

"It better not!"

"Forget it," came a third voice. "We've got enough to do tonight. No sense fighting among ourselves when we've got the Hardys to deal with!"

The men fell silent. Motors began to purr.

"They're probably going to raid the Starfish Marina!" Chet exploded. He dashed from the cottage.

Joe followed him, while Frank rushed to the nearest public phone and called the police. Then he joined Joe, Chet, and Al Hinkley at the marina. They were standing on the jetty counting the lines of boats at anchor.

"They're all accounted for." Hinkley was puzzled. "Are you fellows sure you heard a gang of raiders?"

"I'd like to ask the same question," said a stern voice behind them. It was the constable. "You said boats were being stolen. Well, how many are gone?"

Frank gulped. "It seems like none."

"But there's something fishy about this," Joe burst out. "Half a dozen motors were running."

Frank slapped his forehead with the palm of his hand. "A diversionary tactic. That's what it was! They foxed us into congregating here, while they're making the real hit elsewhere."

"But where?" Chet asked.

"Good night!" Joe exclaimed. "The *Flying Express!* We'd better get over there double-quick!"

They piled into cars and sped to the hydrofoil dock. Spencer Given was standing there, gazing forlornly over the water. Shoulders sagging, he turned toward the group running toward him.

"You're too late!" Given's features contorted with rage. "The *Flying Express* has been stolen!"

CHAPTER XVI

Clever Clues

"I was in my office at the dock when I heard the hydrofoil motors rev up," Given explained. "She was in port all day for minor repairs. I snapped on the lights and came running out to the berth— just in time to see the *Flying Express* vanish."

"Did you get a look at the thieves?" Frank asked. "Could you identify them?"

"No. They were already in the pilot house before I realized what was happening."

"We'll put out an all-points bulletin," the constable promised him. "A hydrofoil's not easy to hide. Yours must be somewhere along the coast not far from here. Someone will spot her."

He went off to sound the alarm, setting in motion an intense search by squad cars and Coast Guard boats. By dawn, however, they all had failed to find the *Flying Express*.

"We don't have any idea where they are," the

134

constable informed Given by telephone. "But we'll keep trying."

Frank, Joe, and Chet, who had joined the search by car, came back with the same disturbing news. Given, wringing his hands, finally went to his lodgings in Providence. The boys remained alone on the dock as the sun began to rise over the bay.

"Is this Malarky's work?" Chet wondered aloud.

"Nothing's impossible where Malarky's concerned," Frank replied. "But we have no evidence tying him to the theft. That's what we need—evidence. Let's look around."

"Any idea what we're looking for?" Chet asked.

"Could be anything. I don't imagine these pirates left a calling card. But maybe they accidentally dropped a clue."

Joe stooped and pulled a greenish paper from between the boards of the dock. "Here's something—a dollar bill! Might not help us with the case, but it'll help fill my piggy bank. Finders keepers!"

The bill was neatly folded. Joe opened it, turned it over, and started to put it in his pocket. Suddenly something caught his eye.

"Frank! Chet!" he called to the others. "There's an odd bit of writing on the reverse side. I can make out a few letters."

The three put their heads together and Joe

pointed to the bottom of the bill where the words ONE DOLLAR were printed in large capitals.

"Take a gander at the N in ONE," he said. "Underneath it somebody has marked the letter I in black pencil. And below that, the letter G."

"Notice this," Frank added. "The first S in STATES has a circle around it. So has the R in AMERICA. Joe, I've got it! Those letters make the initials SR!"

"Sam Radley!" Joe blurted. "He must have dropped the dollar bill to give us a lead!"

"What about the rest of the message?" Chet asked.

Frank studied the bill carefully. "I wonder if we've been trying to read these other letters the wrong way around. Let's try it this way."

He turned the dollar bill lengthwise. "When we put the bald eagle at the top, the N in ONE ceases to be an N. It becomes a Z. Right?"

"Right!" Joe agreed. "And with the I and G we get ZIG!"

"Zigurski!" Frank exclaimed excitedly. "Hooks and his gang grabbed Sam Radley!"

Joe was galvanized. "Let's look around some more," he urged. "Sam may have dropped another clue. He'd want to leave us a clear track to follow."

Finding nothing more on the dock, the boys climbed down a ladder to where the water lapped against the pilings. Paper, sticks, and other debris floated on the tide.

"I think I see something," Frank said. At the bottom of the ladder, he took a firm grip on one rung. Leaning far over he snatched a brown leather object from the water.

"Look, Joe, a wallet!"

They climbed back to the dock. Frank spread the wallet out on his knee. The initials SR were stenciled in gold letters on one flap.

"Sam Radley!" Chet gasped.

"Not much doubt about that," Frank said, "but this will be the final proof."

He carefully slid a number of papers from the inner pocket. They were sodden from their stay in the water, but still legible. Frank extracted a driver's license and held it up for the others to see.

The name Radley was perfectly clear!

Frank looked grim. "Now we're certain that Sam is in the clutches of Hooks Zigurski's gang! And they think Sam is Dad!"

"That means Sam is in real danger!" Chet finished the thought.

"No doubt," Joe said. "But where did the gang take him?"

"My guess is the hydrofoil," Frank said. "Chances are that Sam dropped his wallet into the bay before boarding it to keep his kidnappers from learning his true identity. Could be that they called him Fenton Hardy and he decided to play along with the mistake."

"That means we'd better catch up with the *Flying Express* fast and rescue Sam!"

The sun was well up by now. Word that the hydrofoil was missing had spread in Providence, and curious people came down onto the dock. They buzzed around, exchanging rumors and gossip.

"That's where she was," one man remarked, pointing to the empty berth of the *Flying Express*.

"She must be jinxed," another argued. "She's had too many accidents!"

"Will she ever make the run back to Bayport? Or is she gone for good?" asked a third.

Frank said, "This talk's getting me down. I see Mr. Given has come back. Let's find out if he's learned anything new from the authorities."

Given obviously had not slept. He had dark circles under his eyes and a strained look on his face.

"No," he answered their questions, "I haven't had any further contact with the police or the Coast Guard. For all the good they've done, the *Flying Express* might have vanished from the earth!"

"Still, they've only been on the case for a few hours," Frank pointed out.

"And in the darkness," Joe added.

Chet started to say something about the cor

junction of the planets in Pisces—Given's sign of the Zodiac—but Joe nudged him sharply and whispered, "This is no time to talk astrology!"

Just then Big Malarky came striding up, surrounded by a group of his husky aqualantes. Feet apart and hands on hips, he confronted Given with a mocking smile.

"So," he smirked, "the *Flying Express* has flown the coop! Now isn't that just too bad!"

Given turned purple with rage. "You won't be laughing for long, Malarky! I'm having you arrested on charges of harassment and robbery. You've stolen the *Flying Express!*"

Malarky stopped grinning. "Are you accusing me of being a crook? Why you little punk, I oughta toss you into the bay!"

"Just try it! Just try it!" Given shouted, forgetting his vow never to tangle with his bigger opponent.

Malarky pushed him toward the end of the dock. Chet stepped forward to pull Given back, and took one of Malarky's blows full in the chest. Chet fell over backward, hit his head with a sharp crack on the edge of the dock, and went over into the bay.

"He's unconscious!" someone yelled. "He'll drown!"

Frank and Joe both leaped forward, but a man from the crowd got there before them. Hitting the water in a clean dive, he grabbed Chet and pulled him to the pier. Helped by a dozen willing hands, Chet was lifted onto the dock. There a policeman who had just arrived gave him first aid. When Chet's rescuer climbed out of the water, the Hardy boys gasped. He was Henry Chassen!

"Seems we owe you another debt of gratitude," Joe commented.

Chassen smiled modestly. "Think nothing of it. You were ready to go in after Chet Morton. I just happened to beat you because I was nearer to the scene of the accident. I'm glad to see Chet's coming around."

"We thought you'd left town," Frank said, "since we didn't see you around the Decor Shop. Your landlady didn't know where you were, either."

"I was doing some landscapes of the cape. One day's trip down the coast, that's all."

"You didn't happen to go with Rance Nepo, did you?"

"No. In fact, I understand he's away on his vacation. Why do you ask?"

Frank and Joe explained their suspicion of Nepo. Chassen expressed surprise and added, "I really don't know him very well. I've bought some equipment in his store, but that's about it."

"Oh my head!" Chet groaned. He was sitting up, none the worse except for a bump on his head and a pained expression on his round face.

"Okay, Chet?" Chassen inquired anxiously.

"Okay, thanks to you. I'm told you fished me out of the drink. Remind me to do as much for you someday!"

Frank, Joe, and Chet went back to the cottage, where Chet changed into dry clothes, and Joe phoned Mr. Hardy in Shark Harbor.

"Dad, you were right about Zigurski. Here's the pitch." Joe reported the hydrofoil theft, and the clues they had found in the dock area. "The marked dollar bill and Sam Radley's wallet floating in the bay point to the conclusion that—"

"Hooks Zigurski's gang has Sam Radley!" the Bayport sleuth broke in. "No need to spell it out. We'll have to move fast now. I'll ask the Miami police to put Zigurski under surveillance—if he's still there."

"What do you think we should do at this end?"

"Go to the state prison. Talk to the warden. Since Zigurski did time there, the warden may have a clue about what he's up to."

"Okay, Dad," Frank said. "What'll we do about Sam?"

"Keep mum for a while. Let Zigurski's gang think they have me. It may backfire on them."

"That all, Dad?"

"All for now. And incidentally, my compliments to you and Frank for some expert detective work!"

Frank and Joe hurried to police headquarters

to find out if there were any new developments. There were none.

They were about to leave when they heard a loud commotion. A police escort came in with Big Malarky. He was to be booked on a charge of harassing Given.

The head of the Fidelo Corporation scowled fiercely as the charges were read. Suddenly he raised his hands and stiff-armed the officers on either side of him. They went over like tenpins in a bowling alley.

Malarky lunged for the door, but Frank hit him with a flying tackle, and Joe landed on his shoulders. The policemen pulled the big man to his feet and he stood there foaming with rage.

Turning to the Hardys, he shouted, "I'll get even with you if it's the last thing I ever do!"

CHAPTER XVII

Zodiac Zig

FRANK drove Callie's car to the prison, located in hilly country about fifty miles away.

"I'd hate to try a jailbreak here," Joe commented, pointing to the high walls with watchtowers and armed sentinels.

"Even Hooks Zigurski couldn't escape," Frank said. "He did most of his time and waited for a parole before setting out to get Dad."

The guard on duty at the outer gate examined their credentials. "Fenton Hardy's sons, are you? That name's as good as a free pass. Your father helped us capture an escapee once."

He waved them on through to the administration building. A secretary escorted them into the office of Warden Scott Ogburn, who motioned them to a couple of chairs.

"What can I do for you?" the warden asked.

143

Frank explained. "Sir, it's about a former prisoner who served his time here."

"Name?"

"Zigurski."

The warden smiled grimly. "You boys are playing in a fast league! Hooks Zigurski is one of the most dangerous criminals we've ever had. Sorry I can't introduce you to him. He's out on parole."

"We know that," Joe said, "but Zigurski is a hot suspect in our current case. However, we can't prove anything unless we learn more about him. Perhaps you can give us some inside information."

Warden Ogburn went to a filing cabinet, pulled out a thick manila folder, and began thumbing through a sheaf of papers.

"Zigurski's dossier," he said and briefed the Hardys on the man's background. "When he got out, he went to Miami, Florida," he concluded.

Nothing in the file was new to the boys, and Frank looked disappointed. "Can't you tell us anything about his personality?" he inquired. "Or his friends, for instance?"

"Well," Ogburn said thoughtfully, "Zigurski had a hobby which took up lots of his time here in prison. Astrology."

The young detectives looked at each other in amazement. "If only Chet were here now!" Joe thought. Aloud he said, "Astrology, sir?"

"Yes, Zig was a student of the star and planetary

influences," Ogburn explained. "He was so interested in the signs of the Zodiac that the other prisoners nicknamed him Zodiac Zig. He used to say he wouldn't make a move without consulting his horoscope."

"He was really that serious about astrology?" Frank inquired.

"Come with me and I'll show you how serious he was."

Ogburn led his visitors out of his office, through the administration building, to the cell blocks. Inmates glowered from behind bars as they passed by along the corridor.

The warden conducted the Hardys into an unfurnished cell. "This one hasn't been occupied since Zigurski was here. He certainly left us a memento of his stay. Take a look in this corner."

On the wall was a row of drawings in black ink. "The signs of the Zodiac!" Frank exclaimed.

"They're all accurate," Joe added, "from the rough Y that stands for Aries to the rough H that stands for Pisces."

Ogburn nodded. "Zigurski showed exceptional interest in the subject and, of course, had plenty of spare time to read up on it. Let's go over to the library. You'll see the books he borrowed."

The assistant librarian on duty at the time was a trustee who looked more like a college professor than a convicted forger.

"Zigurski?" he said to them. "I remember him

well. Came in regularly. Always wanted books on astrology, horoscopes, that sort of thing. I even borrowed some books from other libraries for him."

"Did he have a favorite book he read more than the others?" Joe queried.

"Yes, indeed. Here it is." The trustee took a volume from a shelf and handed it over.

Joe looked at the printing on the spine. "It's called *Basic Astrology*." He leafed through the pages. "What sign of the Zodiac did Chet say Zigurski was born under?"

"Cancer," Frank recalled.

Joe found the chapter on Cancerians. Near the heading a note was inscribed in pencil.

It read: *ZIG, Milwaukee, July 20, 11 P.M.*

"That's Zigurski's handwriting," the librarian remarked. He spoke tartly to indicate that he disapproved of borrowers writing in library books.

"Zodiac Zig must have been describing himself," Joe observed. "The place where he was born, the day of the month, and the hour."

Frank agreed. "Take a look through the chapter, Joe, and see what kind of advice he might have gotten from it."

Joe read from the book. " 'A Cancerian is not impulsive. He plans carefully for future action, no matter how long it may take. Being ruled by the moon, the sign of the Crab is favorable to enterprises involving water, especially bays and inlets where the moon governs the tides. He bides his time, and then acts vigorously.' "

Joe closed the book. "That could explain why Zigurski never tried to break jail. He was biding time until his parole."

Frank nodded. "And his horoscope foretold success for his enterprises when he got out. He headed for the coast to set up another racket."

While the boys were talking, another trustee hovered near them on the other side of the row of bookshelves. Pretending to read a book, he listened intently to the remarks about Hooks Zigurski.

Joe noticed him, and was about to say so when the warden spoke. "I'll show you around the prison when you're finished. You can tell your famous father that the criminals he catches are in good hands!"

They left the library and went through the dining room, past the laundry, and into the recreation area. Glancing back, Joe noticed the trustee tagging along. Realizing he had been seen, the man slipped into another room.

When the group moved on, the man reappeared, staying close behind them during the tour of the prison.

Joe decided that the warden ought to know. "We're being shadowed," he said, jerking a thumb in the direction of the trustee.

"Martin?" Ogburn said. "Pay no attention. He

used to be Zigurski's crony. Never gives us any trouble. He's probably on some assignment that brings him to this part of the prison."

The warden pushed open a door. "Here's something we're very proud of—the workshop."

The huge area was abuzz with activity. Convicts were busy with power tools, heavy wrenches, and mechanical screwdrivers. Some were carving pieces of wood into shape for furniture and lawn decorations. Others were fitting parts together to form tables, chairs, bookcases and book ends.

"This is good training for civilian life," Ogburn explained. "Every man has an opportunity to go straight and make a good living when he gets out of here."

Frank was attracted to a shear that no one was using. The long blade hovered motionless above a sheet of metal on the plate beneath. He admired the beautiful clean lines of the machine and leaned over for a better view.

The blade began to move!

"Look out, Frank!" Joe yelled. He grabbed his brother by the arm and hurled him to the floor. Just missing Frank's head, the blade plunged down in a wicked flash of steel biting into steel!

As Frank rose shakily to his feet, Joe looked accusingly at the convicts nearest to the shear.

The warden whirled around and faced them. "Who started that machine?" he demanded.

"Look out, Frank!" Joe yelled

No one answered. There was a scuffling of feet outside the door. Two guards appeared, dragging Martin between them.

"We saw him trip the release and then run out of the room," one guard explained.

"Tell me why you did it!" Ogburn commanded.

The trustee stood with a hangdog look. "I ain't spilling nothing," he spat out viciously.

"Take him to my office," the warden ordered the guards. "Sorry, boys," he said to Frank and Joe. "I was wrong about Martin. Looks as if he's still on Zigurski's side. Anyway, that's one more piece of information you can take back with you."

"I trust Martin isn't due for parole very soon," Frank commented.

"No fear of that," the warden stated emphatically. "He'll be in residence here for a long time!"

"That's some comfort," Joe remarked as he and Frank drove back to the cottage. "Martin's got too much imagination to be loose. Who else would have used a shear as a weapon?"

Frank nodded. "By the way, remind me to give you an assist if you're ever in a hairy situation like that."

"Sure will, Frank. Now let's go over to the marina and give Chet the low-down on Zodiac Zig!"

Chet exploded with excitement when he heard the news. "Jumping Gemini! This changes everything. Now I know what Hooks is going to do!"

Joe was skeptical. "How's that again?"

"Look. Zigurski's birthday is coming up. No Cancerian in his right mind would go into action now. I'll bet you ten to one that Zodiac Zig is lying low until the hour of his birth is over. Right after that would be a good time for him to act and—"

"All right," Joe interrupted, "let's assume that everything stays quiet until his birthday. What happens then?"

"Anything can happen!" Chet declared.

Frank became serious. "This gives us a fix on the timing. Zigurski was born at eleven at night. He may strike around midnight, then. That's when his sign of the Zodiac becomes favorable, and he's not the type to wait any longer than he has to."

Frank went to the phone, dialed Spencer Given, and was informed that no trace of the *Flying Express* had yet been found. Then he put in a call to his father in Shark Harbor.

"Zigurski has dropped out of sight down in Florida," Fenton Hardy reported. "The police tailed him to the Miami airport and lost him. You and Joe get down there and see if you can pick up a clue."

"To Miami?"

"Yes, and as fast as you can."

The Hardys roared away from the cottage in Callie's car, parked it at the Starfish Marina where she could pick it up, caught a taxi to the Providence airport, and flew to Miami.

"We'll check with the reservation clerks first," Joe suggested as the big plane taxied up to the terminal. "Suppose you take the domestic flights, and I'll take the foreign."

They drew a series of blanks until Frank reached the desk of Coastal Airways, a company flying between Miami and Canada. The clerk shook his head at the name Zigurski, but Frank's description of the criminal rang a bell.

"That mechanical right hand!" the man exclaimed. "He took off from here under the name John Read."

"Where did he go?"

"He bought a ticket to Boston."

Frank hustled over to Joe with the news.

"Holy catfish, Frank! We'd better stay right on his heels!"

"Then let's go! We just have time to catch the next flight to Massachusetts!"

The plane zoomed into the air and headed north. The boys unfastened their seat belts, yawned, and settled back for the flight.

A moment later the voice of the pilot came through the loudspeaker. "I'm sorry, ladies and gentlemen, but we're returning to Miami. Please fasten your seat belts and observe the No Smoking sign."

There was no further explanation, but the buzz

of excited chatter among the passengers continued until the pilot landed the jet. Everyone was asked to leave the plane. They were directed to the terminal building, where an airline representative spoke to the group. He apologized for the delay and said, "We had a report that there's a bomb hidden aboard. The plane will be checked immediately."

The passengers gasped.

Joe turned to Frank. "Do you suppose one of Zigurski's men has been trailing us?"

CHAPTER XVIII

A Growing Suspicion

"I'D say so," Frank answered grimly. "Now we're the pursued. Hooks has turned the tables on us."

"Well, his plan succeeded," Joe said glumly. "Except for the bomb scare, we'd be heading into the Boston airport instead of cooling our heels in Miami."

"Better than being blown up in mid-air," Frank observed. "Still, the scare may have been a hoax. Zigurski may want to delay us just long enough for him to pull off his caper."

"Right, Frank. Let's see if the bomb squad found anything aboard the plane."

The baggage had been removed by now, and experts were giving the big jet a thorough going-over. Police and fire vehicles clogged the runway. An airport maintenance truck stood by with a tank full of chemical foam in case of an explosion.

154

"Anything doing?" Frank asked the head of the bomb squad.

"Nothing so far. But I won't sign a bill of health for this plane until every square inch has been searched."

The Hardys walked back to the waiting room.

"Let's give Chet a call," Frank suggested. "We can find out what's happening at the Starfish Marina."

"And we can brief him on what's going on here," Joe added.

They crowded into a pay phone booth. Joe dialed the number. After a moment Chet's voice came on at the other end of the line. Their stocky pal was surprised to hear from them.

"I thought you were in the wild blue yonder. All's quiet here. Whatever excitement there is must be at your end."

"Excitement is right," Joe said, and went on to describe the bomb scare on the plane.

Chet whistled. "Say, that means you're getting hot! You've singed Zodiac Zig's tail feathers, and he's trying to shake you off!"

"That's the way we read it," Frank declared. "But we intend to keep after him."

"How about letting me give you a hand? I've got a few days' leave coming for overtime. Suppose I fly up to Boston as a one-man reinforcement!"

The Hardys willingly agreed. As Joe put it,

"We may have a hot potato on our hands when we corner Zigurski."

Chet chuckled. "Don't forget I'm an expert at dealing with hot potatoes, preferably French fries. Maybe we'd better mash this one!"

Joe laughed. "Mashed Zigurski is a dish I'd like to see. Still, this is no joke, Chet. You'd better come prepared for some rough stuff."

Chet became serious. "Roger. Where shall I meet you?"

Frank and Joe conferred in the booth, and suggested the Boston Airport Motel at 7 A.M. the next morning. Chet promised to be there.

By now the plane had been cleared and reloaded. The passengers went aboard, and the flight north resumed.

"We need Chet," Frank said as he and Joe settled into their seats once again. "If Zig is in Boston, chances are that the *Flying Express* is headed in that direction with Sam Radley. And we don't know how many of Hooks' hoods are with him."

"They've probably arranged a rendezvous along the coast," Joe remarked. "We could run into a gang of toughs. That's the kind of situation when it's nice to see Chet Morton throwing his weight around."

The jet roared on. After a while Frank gestured out the window. "We're having beautiful flying weather, Joe. Just look at Cape Cutlass down there."

Below them, the cape spread out in bright sunlight. Not a cloud blocked their view. They could see every turn and twist of the coast, every cove and inlet, for miles in either direction. The landscape zipped past beneath the wing tips as the plane streaked north.

Joe settled back for a snooze. "Wake me when we get to Boston," he said.

When the plane landed, the Hardys went to the airport motel and turned in early. Next morning there came a knock at the door.

Frank glanced at his watch. "Chet is early. It's only six o'clock."

Joe stepped to the door and flung it open.

"Henry Chassen!" Frank and Joe exclaimed together.

The artist smiled apologetically as he entered. "Sorry to disappoint you. I know you're expecting Chet Morton. I'm substituting for him."

"Anything wrong with Chet?" Joe inquired.

"Nothing at all. He got in touch with me and said he was on to the boat thieves. Felt he should stick with them."

Frank rubbed his chin. "That's the best thing to do in a case like this. When you've got the criminals in sight, keep them in sight."

"How about yourself?" Joe queried.

Chassen spread his hands as if to say the explanation was all quite simple.

"I've just finished my commission for the Decor

Shop. So when Chet asked me to fly up here in his place, I had no reason to say no. Incidentally, he gave me a message for you."

The Hardys leaned forward eagerly.

"Here it is. The trail leads to a town on the Maine coast. Place called High Rock. A deputy police chief is waiting there with a vital clue!"

Frank was excited. "Sounds as if Chet's picked up a lead to the *Flying Express!*"

Joe looked doubtful. Even though Chassen had dispelled their earlier suspicions, he suddenly felt that something might be wrong. Saying he had to make a call, he went to the lobby and dialed the Starfish Marina. Not a sound came through from the other end. Even the operator failed to get a response. Giving up, Joe returned to the motel room.

"Something bothering you?" Henry asked, studying his glum face.

"Well, I tried to call Chet to see if he had any new dope, but couldn't get through to him."

The artist smiled sympathetically. "Don't be alarmed. There was a big storm yesterday in the Cape Cutlass area. Thunder and lightning, and gale-force winds. Knocked out electric and phone services."

"Oh?" Frank asked. "The weather was perfectly clear when we flew over the cape en route to Boston!"

"The storm started later," Chassen explained.

"Well, let's head for High Rock," Frank suggested. "No use wasting time."

The three left the motel and started to walk to a rent-a-car garage on the corner. Frank stopped abruptly.

"Wait a minute," he said. "I've forgotten something. I'll be right back."

Entering the building, he raced up the steps two at a time and went to their room. Seizing a laundry slip, he wrote on the back: *Chet—High Rock, Maine.* He left the piece of paper on the table, weighted with an ashtray. Then he phoned the manager and asked him to let Chet Morton in when he arrived.

"Just in case Chassen's story is phony," Frank thought. Then he rejoined the others and they strode quickly to the rental agency.

Frank took the wheel of the hired car. Joe sat on the opposite side and Chassen in the middle. They made good time heading north from Massachusetts to Maine.

"This is a new experience for me, trailing criminals to their hideout," Chassen remarked cheerfully after a short stop for lunch. "But it must be routine in the Hardy family."

"We've worked on a few cases," Joe admitted.

"We give Dad a hand from time to time," Frank added.

"How's he doing this time?"

Frank spun the wheel, stepped on the gas, and

whizzed around a tractor-trailer in the right lane of the highway. "We've lost touch with him in the past couple of days."

"He's still at Shark Harbor, isn't he?"

Frank frowned. "Maybe yes, maybe no. We just don't know."

"Could be he's figured out the Maine angle," Chassen persisted.

"Could be."

"Let's not jump to conclusions," Joe put in. "Remember Chet's warning! The stars aren't right for hasty judgments!"

A sign with the name High Rock loomed before them.

"Turn here," Chassen advised. "That dirt road will take us to a lane leading to the barn where we're to meet the deputy police chief after dark."

Frank drove about five miles before cutting to the left down the lane. Following Chassen's instructions, he parked under a clump of trees. He turned off the ignition and pocketed the car key.

"Joe and I will take a look around," Frank said. "Get the lay of the land while it's still light."

"Okay," the artist answered. "I'll wait in the car."

A hundred yards into the woods Frank pulled Joe to a halt and muttered, "We're not going back to the car. We can learn more by ourselves. Besides, I don't quite trust our buddy any more."

"Neither do I," Joe replied.

They waited for darkness to fall, and then slipped cautiously through the undergrowth to the barn, a derelict building surrounded by weeds, pitted with woodchuck holes along the foundations.

A sudden glow inside the barn told them that someone had lighted a kerosene lamp. Signaling Joe to follow, Frank crept stealthily up to a window. With bated breath the boys peered over the sill.

Two men faced each other in the dim light. One had a hook instead of a hand—Zigurski!

The other was Henry Chassen!

"All right, brother," Zigurski said harshly, "where's the merchandise?"

Chassen spoke defensively. "They gave me the slip. I don't know where they are, except that they can't be far away."

The reply came like a clap of thunder.

"You stupid Capricorn!"

CHAPTER XIX

Key to a Capture

FRANK and Joe stared at each other. Chassen was in league with Zigurski! But what did the word brother mean? Were the two men related?

Chassen was speaking loudly. "Don't call me stupid! I cut the phone line at the Starfish Marina! I got the two punks up here where we could grab them, didn't I?"

"What d'ya mean grab them?" Zigurski stormed. "You let them get away! I shouldn't have let you handle the job."

"Well, what do we do now?"

"The Hardys will probably tip off the local gumshoes if we don't work fast. We gotta clear out of here. Got the car key?"

Chassen nodded. "I pocketed the duplicate we got from the rental agency."

"Okay, let's make tracks," Zigurski growled. He blew out the kerosene lamp. Darkness settled over

162

the barn. Footsteps thumped across the floor and a door creaked open.

Frank and Joe hastily pulled away from the window. They ran through the woods intending to reach the car first and make their getaway. Behind them they could hear Zigurski and Chassen crashing through the undergrowth in the same direction.

"There's the car!" Joe panted. "Hurry up! They've heard us. They know we're here!"

Frank fought for breath. "Where's—the—key?" Desperately he rummaged around in his pocket until he felt the metal between his fingers. With a sigh of relief he jerked the key out.

Then, with a gasp, he lost his grip on it. The key fell to the ground, disappearing into a tangle of weeds and small bushes.

"No use searching in the dark," he grated. "We'll have to make a run for it!"

Their pursuers pounded after them in a frantic chase down the lane. Frank and Joe heard the roar of an approaching motorcycle. Catching them in the glare of his headlight, the cyclist came hurtling to meet them. His tires squealed as the rider skidded to a halt, removed his crash helmet, and jumped off.

Chet Morton! His round, freckled face broke into a grin. "I found your message! Zoomed right up here on my trusty rented bike! Seems as if I arrived just in the nick of time. What's up?"

"Douse that light!" Frank hissed.

Chet seemed mystified. "What in the world—?"

"Let's get out of here," Joe interrupted, jumping onto the rear seat. Frank squeezed in behind him. Chet, realizing that the situation was serious, frantically tried to start the bike. The engine would not turn over!

"Try again!" Frank urged.

But before Chet could get the engine going, Zigurski and Chassen were on them. Jumped from behind, Frank and Joe were handcuffed before they could defend themselves.

Chet leaped off his motorcycle and charged the assailants. He bowled Chassen over, and was giving a good account of himself when Zigurski's steel claw clamped around his wrist. It twisted his arm behind his back until he groaned with pain.

Keeping a tight grip on Chet, the ex-con snapped orders. Chassen pulled the motorcycle up on its wheels and rolled it behind a pile of underbrush. Producing the duplicate key, he walked to the car, got in, and started the motor.

"All right, brother," he called out. "I'm ready for the ride whenever you are."

"Half brother," Zigurski snarled. "Don't make our relationship closer than it is!"

"Well, is this a family quarrel or isn't it?" Joe needled them.

Chassen glared. "Maybe I should have taken

care of you earlier. Like when I drilled a hole in the fuel tank of your plane and made you come down on the beach. Or when you were stone-cold in the boathouse."

"Why didn't you?" Frank challenged.

"Our plans called for me to be friendly with you until we were ready to make our move," Chassen said shortly.

"Which is why you hauled me out of the drink," Chet stated.

"Right. No harm in letting you know the truth now."

Zigurski turned to Joe. "You—get in the back." Then Zodiac Zig forced Chet next to Frank, and wedged himself in last of all.

Chassen started the car. They rode down the lane to the dirt road, and on toward the highway.

Chet broke the silence. "Now I know how a fish feels when a lobster gets a claw on it," he complained.

Zigurski sneered. "That's what you get for poking your nose into my affairs. I only brought two pairs of handcuffs, enough to take care of the Hardys. I'll have to hang on to you myself."

He tightened his grip as he spoke. Chet winced. "I'd just as soon keep my arm if you don't mind," he said ruefully. "I'm quite attached to it."

Zigurski merely snickered. The boys got a good look at their captor for the first time.

He had a thick shock of blond hair and a deep scar across his forehead. His pale-blue eyes moved constantly as if to indicate he trusted no one.

Zigurski had heavy shoulders and muscular arms. His one good hand opened and closed as he flexed the muscles. He settled back with a pleased expression on his face. "Everything's going according to the book," he exulted.

"The book on basic astrology?" Joe asked.

"How did you know about that? Well, it's all there. The stars are right for me and wrong for you. It's great to be a Cancerian!"

Chassen turned onto the highway and looked at Zigurski in the front mirror. "Be careful of Morton. He's a Cancerian too."

"Oh yeah?" Zigurski was impressed. He considered the point for a moment before relaxing. "You can't rely on the stars to do everything," he told Chet. "You gotta work with them. You must have done something stupid to put yourself in this fix."

Chet assumed a solemn look. "Suppose we go back to Cape Cutlass and consult my horoscope."

"Is that supposed to be a joke? Cape Cutlass is out. I've got the Hardys, and I've got you too, for a bonus."

"Where are we going?" Frank asked.

"To the *Flying Express*. I have a surprise waiting for you."

Chassen suddenly speeded up and swerved past

a patrol car. Joe could see in the mirror that it was following them.

"Take a chance!" he thought. "It may be the last one!"

Violently he threw himself against the door, reaching for the handle with his manacled hands, desperate to attract the attention of the officers in the patrol car.

Chassen grasped his collar and dragged him back, twisting until Joe gasped for breath.

Had the officers spotted the struggle in the car ahead of them? Apparently not. The mirror showed them turning off the highway.

Joe slumped dejectedly in his seat.

Zigurski chuckled. "See what I mean? The stars are never wrong!"

Everyone in the car fell silent now as Chassen drove north along the coastal highway of eastern Maine. Finally he turned into a lane leading down to the beach. Then he switched off his lights and continued on under a full moon.

"We should be near," Chassen commented.

"We are," Zigurski agreed. "That's it over there." He pointed to a mound that resembled a huge rock rising out of the water offshore.

Chassen parked the car. The five got out and walked across the sand. As they drew near the mound, the rocklike image dissolved. It was clever camouflage made of painted wood and canvas! Behind the camouflage a hydrofoil rode at anchor.

"So we've finally located the *Flying Express!*" Joe muttered.

"Too bad we can't pass the word to Mr. Given," Frank replied.

A launch carried the group to the hydrofoil. Henry Chassen bowed to the three prisoners when they stepped onto the deck. "Welcome aboard," he mocked them. Several members of the gang were already there, busily preparing for a voyage.

"Before we sail, comes the surprise," Chassen sneered. "This is on me. I made the identification from the snapshot you so unwisely showed me."

"Bring out the fuzz Hardy," Zigurski commanded. "Boys, here's your famous father!"

A couple of strong-arm men pushed a man out of the pilot house. He looked pale and haggard from ill-treatment, but he raised his head without flinching.

"Hello, Sam," Frank said quietly.

Zigurski's jaw dropped. He struggled to say something. Finally words came out." Wh-what—?"

"Happy birthday, Mr. Zigurski!" chortled Chet Morton.

CHAPTER XX

End of the Road

ZIGURSKI released Chet and whirled savagely on Chassen. The steel claw flashed out. Chassen cringed as it gripped his arm.

Bellowing like an enraged bull, Zigurski dragged his screaming half brother to the rail and pitched him over the side.

"What's up, Zig?" someone asked.

"That idiot grabbed the wrong man at Shark Island. This isn't Hardy you've been holding! It's the guy who works for him!"

Water splashed along the hull of the hydrofoil. Chassen was struggling to climb back. His hand slipped and the crew rushed to help him.

The commotion gave Chet a chance to escape. Leaping onto the rail at the opposite side of the *Flying Express,* he dived in and began to swim underwater toward shore.

Zigurski heard him hit the water. "Stop him!" Zig shouted furiously. "Plug him when he comes up for air!"

Rifles were quickly handed out of the pilot house and three of the crew began shooting.

"They're getting too close for Chet's safety!" Frank whispered to Joe and Sam as the fusillade churned up the water. "Let's make it a little harder for them!"

Stepping forward, he jarred the elbow of one of the marksmen. "Sorry to spoil your aim," he murmured sarcastically.

Following Frank's lead, Joe and Sam bumped into the two other thugs with rifles. Their shots went wild. Cursing their captives, they reloaded their weapons.

Too late! Chet staggered from the surf, rushed ashore, and threw himself behind some driftwood.

Joe taunted Zigurski. "Is this your big surprise? Arranging a get-together with Sam Radley?"

Zig scowled. "I was gonna ship your nosy old man to Siberia. Now Radley'll be making the trip with the Hardy boys for an escort!"

"You'll never get away with it," Frank retorted. "Siberia is quite a distance from Maine!"

Zigurski grinned wickedly. "Yeah, but a trawler from Siberia is fishing just a few miles out in Canadian waters. We'll make the transfer from the hydrofoil to the trawler tonight. And by morning you'll be on your way!"

A beam of light stabbed through the darkness.

"Morton's reached the car!" Zigurski screamed. "He's turned on the emergency blinker lights! Smash 'em or we'll have the Coast Guard on our backs!"

Shots rang out and bullets kicked up puffs of sand near the car. Chet started the engine and drove the vehicle down the beach. He turned sharply and careened to a stop beside a large boulder.

"It's safer here," he told himself as slugs caromed off the boulder. "And I can still work these blinker lights. If only the Coast Guard spots them!"

Zigurski raged around the deck of the hydrofoil, cursing Chassen, the crew, and the captives. Then, calming down, he gave orders to start the vessel. Down came the camouflage of canvas and wood. The motor started to purr. The *Flying Express* moved away from the shore, picking up speed.

Joe nudged Frank and pointed over the stern to a speedboat in the distance. "Rescuers?" he asked.

"Affirmative!" Frank answered. "They can't miss Chet's blinkers."

"But they'll never catch up!" said a triumphant voice behind them. Zigurski had overheard the conversation. "This boat will run away from anybody!" he bragged.

Poking his head into the pilot house, he

snapped an order. "Full speed ahead!" The *Flying Express* rapidly widened the gap between it and its pursuer. The gang's attention was centered on making a getaway and the three captives were momentarily forgotten.

Frank motioned to Joe and Sam. "We've got to stop the hydrofoil," he urged. "I have an idea. Let's bombard the foils with life preservers!"

"I get it!" Joe said excitedly. "We'll snarl the propellers!"

Sam nodded. "The props are close to the surface since we're riding so high without cargo. I'll create a diversion," he promised, "while you two start pitching!"

Darting to the front deck, Sam tackled one of the crew. The others pounced on him. A battle royal raged near the pilot house.

As quickly as their handcuffs would allow, Frank and Joe pulled life jackets with attached ropes from their niches along the rail. They took aim at the frothy water below and threw—and missed.

Frantically they ripped down more preservers. The next pair missed, and the next. No time left. The crew, realizing what they were up to, came barreling down on them.

Desperately Frank made one last throw. A rope caught in the whirling mechanism of the propeller and the life preserver whipped into the blade. Suddenly the blade snapped!

The hydrofoil lost momentum and the hull settled down in the water. The speedboat rapidly drew near. A helicopter came buzzing overhead, and a voice called through a bullhorn, warning the criminals that men of the Coast Guard were coming aboard.

Zigurski and his gang surrendered without offering any resistance. "No use fighting the stars!" Zigurski complained. "What's wrong with the Zodiac, anyway?"

"Nothing," Joe retorted. "But there's a lot wrong with Zodiac Zig!"

A Coast Guard frogman replaced the broken propeller with a blade from the *Flying Express* spare-parts locker. Then the officer in charge ordered his pilot to chart a course to Portland.

Meanwhile the prisoners were handcuffed and informed of their legal rights. Seeing that the game was over, Zig readily answered the boys' questions.

"Yeah," he said, "I've been running the racket along the coast. Skee only pulled off jobs when I gave him orders!"

"How did the hydrofoil fit into your plans?" Joe wanted to know.

"Ask my smart brother!"

Chassen looked completely deflated as he spoke. "Big Malarky wanted the *Flying Express* out of the way. He asked me to get rid of it."

"And you took the problem to Zig?" Frank said.

Chassen shrugged. "Zig's the strong-arm member of the family!"

"I wanted to kill two birds with one stone," Zigurski spoke up. "I was gonna grab Fenton Hardy, and make him pay for sending me up. When my men stole the *Flying Express,* I gave them orders to kidnap Hardy."

"All the loose ends tied up in a neat package," Sam Radley observed.

After seeing the prisoners locked up in jail the next day, Frank, Joe, Chet, and Sam flew to Cape Cutlass. Mr. Hardy was at the cottage near the Starfish Marina along with Callie and Iola. He was greatly relieved to hear of Radley's rescue.

Frank and Joe quickly described the recovery of the *Flying Express* and the capture of Zodiac Zig and his gang.

"Great work," Mr. Hardy praised them. "Meanwhile, I've rounded up Hooks' group at Shark Island and here, with some ingenious and unexpected help from the girls!"

Frank and Joe were surprised. "How so?" Frank asked.

"We saw Rance Nepo sneaking out of the cellar of the Decor Shop," Callie explained. "No one in the shop knew he was there. But we blew the whistle on him! The cop on the beat nabbed him when he tried to flee."

"Nepo put our jackets on the dummies," Iola added. "He thought we'd all be so mystified that we'd miss the hydrofoil trip back to Bayport. And without the Hardy boys on board, his pals could do in the *Flying Express*."

Fenton Hardy took up the account. "Malarky was responsible for the plane that dropped the log in front of the hydrofoil, and for the boat that got cut in two. In fact, you can chalk up a lot of skulduggery to him!"

"Such as the bulldozer that nearly ran us down in the cabin?" Frank inquired.

"And the fire at the dock that threw a scare into Given and his customers?" Joe guessed.

"Right on both counts."

"What about the disappearing outboard motors in the garage?" Frank continued.

"That was Zigurski's doing. He laid all the plans for the thievery. Also, it was his idea to plant Chassen in our camp as a spy."

Joe nodded. "And to think that we trusted that jerk in the beginning!"

Frank got up. "That reminds me. We'd better go over to Mr. Given's office and tell him the good news about the *Flying Express*."

Joe placed a hand on his arm. "There's one mystery that hasn't been cleared up. Sam, what's the story on those twenty-year-old license plates we saw in the boathouse where they held us prisoner?"

Sam Radley smiled. "You won't believe this, but they were issued to your Aunt Gertrude!"

The boys gaped. "You've got to be kidding!" Joe said.

"No, it's the truth," Sam replied.

Mr. Hardy burst out laughing. "Wait till Gertrude finds out she's involved in this mystery! She won't believe it!"

"Imagine Aunty being investigated by us!" Frank said. "Boy! That's funny!"

Mr. Hardy shook his head. "My sister was quite a driver in her day," he said. "In a ladylike way of course. She had her own car, I remember it clearly. A bright-green sedan. Washed it every other day. Come to think of it, she even got a summons once."

"For speeding?" Joe asked.

"No. She was driving too slow on the turnpike!"

When the laughter subsided, Mr. Hardy turned to Sam. "Tell us, Sam, how did you track down the license plates?"

"Well," Sam Radley began, "first I tried the Bureau of Motor Vehicles. They couldn't find any record of them. They were destroyed in a fire years ago. Finally, through a friend, I located a man whose hobby is collecting discarded license plates. As a boy, he found Miss Hardy's plates in a trash can, where she had deposited them."

"He didn't by any chance own the boathouse?" Joe prodded.

"Well, he did for a while. That was when he

put the plates on the cabinet door where you saw them. He left them when he sold the place, and nobody bothered to take them down after that."

"That's a funny twist to the mystery," Joe said. But their next adventure, *The Clue of the Broken Blade,* was to be anything but humorous.

Frank had one last query. "You found the boathouse, didn't you, Sam?"

"Yes I did."

"Is there a red neon sign near it?"

"Not a neon sign, but one with red incandescent bulbs which road construction companies use. A new highway is being built in that area. The warning sign is large and that's why you spotted the glow beyond the boathouse."

"What does it say?"

Sam chuckled. "It says *End of Road.*"

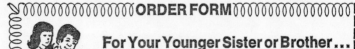

ORDER FORM

For Your Younger Sister or Brother...

The Bobbsey Twins

from the publishers of Nancy Drew & The Hardy Boys

Meet Freddie, Flossie, Nan and Bert, the two sets of twins, as they go from one exciting adventure to another. To make it easy for members of your family to purchase Bobbsey Twins Books, we've enclosed this handy order form.

48 TITLES AT YOUR BOOKSELLER OR COMPLETE AND MAIL THIS HANDY COUPON TO:

GROSSET & DUNLAP, INC.

P.O. Box 941, Madison Square Post Office, New York, N.Y. 10010
Please send me the Bobbsey Twins Adventure Book(s) checked below @ $2.95 each, plus 25¢ *per book* postage and handling. My check or money order for $_____ is enclosed.

☐ 1. Of Lakeport 8001-X	☐ 47. At Big Bear Pond 8047-8
☐ 2. Adventure in the Country .. 8002-8	☐ 48. On A Bicycle Trip 8048-6
☐ 3. Secret at the Seashore 8003-6	☐ 49. Own Little Ferryboat 8049-4
☐ 4. Mystery at School 8004-4	☐ 50. At Pilgrim Rock 8050-8
☐ 5. At Snow Lodge 8005-2	☐ 51. Forest Adventure 8051-6
☐ 6. On A Houseboat 8006-0	☐ 52. London Tower 8052-4
☐ 7. Mystery at Meadowbrook ... 8007-9	☐ 53. In the Mystery Cave 8053-2
☐ 8. Big Adventure at Home 8008-7	☐ 54. In Volcano Land 8054-0
☐ 9. Search in the Great City ... 8009-5	☐ 55. And the Goldfish Mystery .. 8055-9
☐ 10. On Blueberry Island 8010-9	☐ 56. And the Big River Mystery .. 8056-7
☐ 11. Mystery on the Deep Blue	☐ 57. The Greek Hat Mystery 8057-5
Sea 8011-7	☐ 58. Search for the Green
☐ 12. Adventure in Washington ... 8012-5	Rooster 8058-3
☐ 13. Visit to the Great West 8013-3	☐ 59. And Their Camel
☐ 14. And the Cedar Camp	Adventure 8059-1
Mystery 8014-1	☐ 60. Mystery of the King's
☐ 15. And The Country Fair	Puppet 8060-5
Mystery 8015-X	☐ 61. And the Secret of Candy
☐ 16. Camping Out 8016-8	Castle 8061-3
☐ 17. Adventures With Baby	☐ 62. And the Doodlebug
May 8017-6	Mystery 8062-1
☐ 18. And the Play House	☐ 63. And the Talking Fox
Secret 8018-4	Mystery 8063-X
☐ 19. And the Four-Leaf Clover	☐ 64. The Red, White and Blue
Mystery 8019-2	Mystery 8064-8
☐ 20. The Mystery at Cherry	☐ 65. Dr. Funnybone's Secret 8065-6
Corners 8020-6	☐ 66. The Tagalong Giraffe 8066-4
☐ 24. Wonderful Winter Secret ... 8024-9	☐ 67. And the Flying Clown 8067-2
☐ 25. And the Circus Surprise ... 8025-7	☐ 68. On the Sun-Moon Cruise ... 8068-0
☐ 27. Solve A Mystery 8027-3	☐ 69. The Freedom Bell Mystery.. 8069-9
	☐ 70. And the Smoky Mountain
	Mystery 8070-2

SHIP TO:

☐ 71. The Bobbsey Twins in a TV Mystery Show   8071-0

NAME_____

(please print)

ADDRESS_____

CITY_____STATE_____ZIP_____

Printed in U.S.A.

ORDER FORM

HARDY BOYS MYSTERY SERIES
by Franklin W. Dixon

57 TITLES AT YOUR BOOKSELLER OR COMPLETE AND MAIL THIS HANDY COUPON TO:

GROSSET & DUNLAP, INC.
P.O. Box 941, Madison Square Post Office, New York, N.Y. 10010
Please send me the Hardy Boys Mystery and Adventure Book(s) checked below @ $2.95 each, plus 25¢ *per book* postage and handling. My check or money order for $_____ is enclosed.

1. Tower Treasure	8901-7	28. The Sign of the Crooked Arrow	8928-9
2. House on the Cliff	8902-5	29. The Secret of the Lost Tunnel	8929-7
3. Secret of the Old Mill	8903-3	30. Wailing Siren Mystery	8930-0
4. Missing Chums	8904-1	31. Secret of Wildcat Swamp	8931-9
5. Hunting for Hidden Gold	8905-X	32. Crisscross Shadow	8932-7
6. Shore Road Mystery	8906-8	33. The Yellow Feather Mystery	8933-5
7. Secret of the Caves	8907-8	34. The Hooded Hawk Mystery	8934-3
8. Mystery of Cabin Island	8908-4	35. The Clue in the Embers	8935-1
9. Great Airport Mystery	8909-2	36. The Secrets of Pirates Hill	8936-X
10. What Happened At Midnight	8910-6	37. Ghost at Skeleton Rock	8937-8
11. While the Clock Ticked	8911-4	38. Mystery at Devil's Paw	8938-6
12. Footprints Under the Window	8912-2	39. Mystery of the Chinese Junk	8939-4
13. Mark on the Door	8913-0	40. Mystery of the Desert Giant	8940-8
14. Hidden Harbor Mystery	8914-9	41. Clue of the Screeching Owl	8941-6
15. Sinister Sign Post	8915-7	42. Viking Symbol Mystery	8942-4
16. A Figure in Hiding	8916-6	43. Mystery of the Aztec Warrior	8943-2
17. Secret Warning	8917-3	44. Haunted Fort	8944-0
18. Twisted Claw	8918-1	45. Mystery of the Spiral Bridge	8945-9
19. Disappearing Floor	8919-X	46. Secret Agent on Flight 101	8946-7
20. Mystery of the Flying Express	8920-3	47. Mystery of the Whale Tattoo	8947-5
21. The Clue of the Broken Blade	8921-1	48. The Arctic Patrol Mystery	8948-3
22. The Flickering Torch Mystery	8922-X	49. The Bombay Boomerang	8949-1
23. Melted Coins	8923-3	50. Danger on Vampire Trail	8950-5
24. Short-Wave Mystery	8924-6	51. The Masked Monkey	8951-3
25. Secret Panel	8925-4	52. The Shattered Helmet	8952-3
26. The Phantom Freighter	8926-2	53. The Clue of the Hissing Serpent	8953-X
27. Secret of Skull Mountain	8927-0	54. The Mysterious Caravan	8954-8
		55. The Witchmaster's Key	8955-6
		56. The Jungle Pyramid	8956-4
		57. The Firebird Rocket	8957-2

SHIP TO:

NAME _____
(please print)

ADDRESS _____

CITY _____ STATE _____ ZIP _____

Printed in U.S.A.   **Please do not send cash.**

DETACH ALONG DOTTED LINE AND MAIL IN ENVELOPE WITH PAYMENT